ONE EMPIRE NIGHT

LOST KINGS MC #9.5

AUTUMN JONES LAKE

AHEAD OF THE PACK, LLC

ONE EMPIRE NIGHT (Lost Kings MC #9.5)

Digital ISBN: 978-1-943950-26-3
Print ISBN: 978-1-943950-27-0
Cover Design: Letitia Hasser, RBA Designs
Cover Photo: Adobe Stock
Formatted by: Autumn Jones Lake

Publisher's Notes:

SOCIAL MEDIA

Keep in touch with Autumn!

http://www.autumnjoneslake.com
Book Bub
Goodreads
Instagram
Facebook
Twitter
E-mail: AutumnJLake@gmail.com

LOST KINGS MC

Reading Order

Slow Burn (Lost Kings MC #1)
Corrupting Cinderella (Lost Kings MC #2)
Three Kings, One Night (Lost Kings MC #2.5)
Strength From Loyalty (Lost Kings MC #3)
Tattered on My Sleeve (Lost Kings MC #4)
White Heat (Lost Kings MC #5)
Between Embers (Lost Kings MC #5.5)
Bullets and Bonfires (Stand Alone in the Lost Kings MC World)
More Than Miles (Lost Kings MC #6)
White Knuckles (Lost Kings MC #7)
Beyond Reckless (Lost Kings MC #8)
Beyond Reason (Lost Kings MC #9)
One Empire Night (Lost Kings MC #9.5)

Coming Soon:

After Burn (Lost Kings MC #10)

Zero Tolerance (Lost Kings MC #11)

White Lies (Lost Kings MC #12)

ACKNOWLEDGMENTS

Thank you to my wonderful readers! *One Empire Night* is for you.

I also have to thank Andrea for taking an early look at *One Empire Nigh*t. Jezzie for reviewing it. My crit partners, Cara, Kari, and Virginia who took time out of their own busy writing schedules to read *One Empire Night* and catch all those pesky little errors I miss. If there's any left, that's all me.

Letitia who created a beautiful cover for me with very little notice. Thank you so much!

Thank you to my friend, Jeanette Grey, whose stories about her own adorable tiny human inspired some of Alexa's antics.

Thanks to my Lost Kings MC ladies who helped me share the cover and posted about the release of *One Empire Night*. Your support means everything!

DEDICATION

At some point in life the world's beauty becomes enough.

-Toni Morrison

CHAPTER ONE

MURPHY

"ARE YOU SURE THAT'S GOING TO FIT?" TELLER ASKS, STARING at the monster Fraser fir in front of us.

"That's what she said," I quip. "Or *doesn't* say in your case."

He gives me a hard shove sideways. "I'm serious, asshole."

"Would it be easier if we got a ruler and you two just whipped 'em out?" Charlotte asks in a bored tone.

"Ewwww!" Heidi shrieks. "For the love of God, Charlotte. Why?"

"Nah, I don't want to make him feel bad about himself so close to Christmas," I answer.

Teller holds up a hand, stopping Charlotte from

whatever comeback she has in mind. "Focus, children." He lifts his chin at Heidi. "You sure Rock's okay with this?"

"He wanted to come with us," Heidi says. This is true, but I also know Rock's planning to take Hope away for the weekend and we're running out of time to get this tree up. Having the tree in the living room, mostly decorated when they return will be a nice surprise.

"We'll finish decorating it with them," I assure Heidi.

"We can just put up the one at our house. You guys can stay with us for Christmas," Charlotte offers.

Heidi shifts, uncomfortable I think, with the offer and I understand why. I wrap an arm around her shoulder and pull her to my side. "Next year we'll be in our own house, beautiful," I say in a lower voice.

Not that Rock and Hope ever make us feel unwelcome, but sometimes it's weird we don't have our own place. Like now, when Marcel keeps questioning whether we have permission to put up a damn tree. But I also remember how unhappy he was last year when Alexa celebrated her first Christmas in Alaska, so I let his badgering slide.

"We can do that," Heidi hedges. "Hope said she was looking forward to having a tree in the house this year, though."

"Two trees, coming right up," Charlotte says, pushing past Teller to shake one of the branches. She points at another full, green fir a few feet away. "Get chopping, boys."

"Where's Wrath when you need him?" I grumble. "He's a damn tree-chopping wizard."

"Quit your whining," Teller says, opening the back door of his truck to grab a chainsaw.

Heidi takes Alexa from me. "I'm going to sit in the truck with her." She leans up and gives me a quick kiss on the cheek. "Please don't cut off anything important."

"Be careful, Marcel," Charlotte calls out as she follows Heidi and Alexa.

When they're inside the truck, Marcel pulls out his phone to check his texts.

"He done yet?"

"Not even close," he answers, tucking the phone away. "We'll take our time going home."

"You're not going to the party tonight?"

He blows out a breath. "Charlotte said she didn't mind, but fuck me, I'd rather not. I told Z if we came, it would be late."

"Why? It'll be one big orgy by then."

"Rock's there. He's not gonna let it get out of control." He nods at the first tree. "Stop trying to weasel your way out of some manual labor."

"What're you talking about? I've been working my ass off since dawn, you dick."

Teller grins and wields the chainsaw around like a horror-movie villain.

"Overcompensating much?"

He sets the chainsaw on the tailgate, then throws me some safety gear. "Let's get this done. I have ornaments and stuff from my grandmother's in the storage unit. We can stop there on the way home and pull them out for Heidi."

"Why do you still have stuff stored there?"

"I didn't know if Heidi would want it after she got

settled. I should probably clear it out and store the shit at my place now."

"I got time this week if you want to do it by the end of the month."

"Thanks." He stops and sizes up the tree in front of us. "First things first. Let's get my niece her first Christmas tree."

CHAPTER TWO

ROCK

"Are you sure you don't mind we had to take the truck tonight?" Hope asks.

I glance at her, my gaze traveling over the woven material covering her legs. "The tights you're wearing make up for it."

"It's such a nice night." She lightly touches her fingertips against her window. "Cold but clear and so pretty."

This time I reach over and rest my hand on her knee, giving her a gentle squeeze. "Miss it?"

"A little."

"I don't think you want to show up to this thing all windblown."

"True." She huffs. "I don't want to go at *all*. If it wasn't for Mara, I wouldn't."

"This is the last event she had to organize for the Bar Association, right?"

She laughs. "She's thrilled her term is almost finished. I don't think she expected volunteering for a position on the executive board to be so much work. But it helped her do some networking for Damon's next campaign."

"What's Damon planning to run for now?"

"The vacant Senate seat."

I paid more attention to state politics than you'd think and knew the seat had been vacant since the last senator was arrested for corruption. Damon's too honorable to be bribed—not that I'd try that angle with a friend of Hope's anyway—but the idea of knowing yet another person in New York State government is appealing. In fact, I'm more interested in attending this holiday party for the Empire County Bar Association than the party my club is throwing at Crystal Ball later tonight.

"We'll have to be sure to make a donation to his campaign."

Out of the corner of my eye, I catch Hope swivel her head to stare at me. "I don't think he needs our money."

"Maybe *the club* will make a donation."

"Planning to act as a legislative liaison between motorcyclists and our elected officials, are you?"

I run the hand resting on her leg up her thigh, pushing her skirt higher. "Feeling sassy tonight, Baby Doll?"

Her breath hitches, but she stops my exploration by

pressing her hands against her skirt. "I don't have any extra tights with me."

Actually, I have a whole bag packed for her in the back of my SUV. Hope doesn't know that after our evening out, I'm taking her to a hotel for our own personal holiday celebration.

A gift to *myself* for pasting on my presidential smile and enduring a whole lot of socializing tonight, instead of staying home with my woman the way I'd prefer.

"Turn here," she says pointing to the narrow, one-way street where the Bar Association's office is located. "I assume you don't want anyone parking your car."

"Fuck no."

She chuckles as I pull into the last spot available on the street.

"Wait for me." I step into the crisp night and hurry to her side. Before we left, she'd draped her coat over the back seat. I grab it before opening her door.

Then almost lose my mind when she twists in her seat, angling her leg down to touch the running board.

"What's wrong?" she asks, concern heightening the pitch of her voice.

Meeting her confused green eyes, I groan. She's already nervous about tonight, I don't need her getting the wrong idea. "You're sexy as fuck in that little red dress, lacy tights and tiny boots. I'm starting to think we should go home instead."

I offer my hand and she steps the rest of the way out of the truck.

"Oh." Under the glow of the nearby street lamp she runs

her hands over her hips, down her stomach, to her thighs, fixing the skirt of her dress. "You think it's too sexy? I wasn't sure what would work for both events."

"Baby Doll," I say, holding her coat out for her to slip into, "I'd make you wear a burlap sack every time you leave the house if I thought you wouldn't slice my balls off."

Her husky laughter works me up even more. She reaches for my cheek, her soft, warm fingers resting there for a second. "Lucky for you I don't have a ball-slicing bone in my body."

"Yeah? So where do we stand on the burlap sack?"

More laughter that really makes me consider taking her directly to the hotel. Instead, I offer my arm and she slips hers through, gripping my bicep. "You okay to walk?"

She glances down at her black ankle boots. "It's a short heel. I'll be fine as long as there's no ice."

Her grip tightens as we navigate the uneven sidewalk. Outside the building a number of people have congregated on the sidewalk to talk and smoke. Someone calls out her name.

"Hi, Ross!" she answers, hurrying toward her friend.

He gives me a quick glance before wrapping her up in a short embrace. "How've you been?" He pulls back, eyeing her from head to toe. "Damn, you look good, girl."

"Thank you." She chuckles nervously and takes my hand again. "Have you seen Mara yet?"

"Inside, running around like a mad woman."

"She's thrilled her term is almost up."

"True. She's done such a good job." He lowers his voice.

"I have inside information Angie wants to ask her to run again," he answers.

Since I don't have anything to add to their conversation, I let my attention wander to the small crowd. It's how I'm the first one to spot Adam and his friend approaching. He notices me and lifts his chin. "Hey, Rock." He shakes my hand, then gives Hope a quick hug, barely acknowledging Ross.

"Hope, you haven't met Trooper Tom, have you?" Adam asks, introducing his boyfriend.

Hope raises an eyebrow. "Trooper Tom? Is that because you're a trooper for putting up with this guy?" she teases.

I actually recognize Tom as a State Trooper and stifle a laugh.

Adam finishes the introductions—and explanation for Hope. Tom shakes my hand slowly and gives me a curious once-over. He recognizes me too. Not a surprise since it had been the NYS Troopers who arrested me two summers ago. Could've even been his barracks, although I don't remember him as one of the officers who questioned me.

Hope seems blissfully unaware of the situation and I want to keep it that way. "Should we go inside to find Mara?" I suggest.

"Sure. Nice to meet you, Tom," Hope says.

Ross tags along with us. "Flying solo tonight?" I ask as we climb a short, steep set of stairs into the building.

"Yup. Planning to make the rounds and head out to a much *different* kind of party."

Hope chuckles. "So are we."

Ross waggles his eyebrows and Hope shakes her head.

"Perv." She touches my arm. "We have the club's Christmas party at Crystal Ball later."

His gaze swings back to me. "Two *very* different events indeed."

"Yeah," I agree.

"When are you going to have some male strippers in that joint, Rock? You'd probably make a fortune."

"Actually, Z's been working on a couple different special events for off-nights."

"Nice. Keep me updated."

Hope blinks up at me. "Really?"

Her question amuses me. "Why you wanna see some male strippers?"

Next to us, Ross snorts. "I don't see Miss Innocent going to one of those."

A pretty flush stains Hope's cheeks and she shakes her head. "Why would I need to—" she runs her hand over my chest "—when I have my very own beefcake at home?"

Ross flicks his gaze at me and smirks. "I see your point." He lifts his chin at Hope. "I'm going to circulate. You good?"

"I'm fine. Do you know where Mara is?"

He surveys the crowded room. "A night without the kiddo? I'm guessing Damon used his tie to gag her and they're busy fucking in a closet right about now."

"Ugh, you're awful." Hope gives him a playful shove. "Go hustle the crowd."

Hope

ROCK'S rumbling laughter vibrates against my back and his warm hand strays to the curve of my ass. "What's so funny?"

"Nothing at all." He leans down, whispering against my ear, "Want to go find our own closet?"

"Here? In a building full of lawyers? I'm dry as a desert." This is a lie. I've been turned on from the second Rock stepped out of our room in his gray suit, complete with red tie. On the other hand, that familiar, uneasy flutter stirs in my belly and I hate having Rock here to witness all my awkwardness around my colleagues. Especially since he's always so at ease no matter where he goes.

Believe it or not, I'm actually looking forward to the party at Crystal Ball later. Who knew I'd ever feel more comfortable around a club full bikers and half-naked dancers than in my own world?

"I bet if I checked, I'd discover you're lying." The shiver that works through my body has nothing to do with the cold and everything to do with his low, seductive voice. "Fine, let's go." I tug on his hand to emphasize my desire to leave.

He groans and tightens his hold on me. "Nice try. You have to say hello to Mara. And you're supposed to talk to at least three people before I can allow you to leave."

Why did I ever share my silly rules for socializing at these things with him? "Adam, Ross, Tom—"

"And not your friends."

Mara's voice stops me from growling out my annoyance and I turn to find her trotting down the large staircase to our left.

"Hi!"

I hurry over to meet her and give her a quick hug. "Everything looks great."

"Thank you."

My gaze narrows, giving her a more critical look. "Honey, your lipstick's smudged."

"Oh, shit." She lets out a nervous giggle and I dig in my purse for a compact and hand it to her.

I step back, examining her a little closer. The green dress she's wearing has a fitted top that both accents her assets and frames her flushed chest. "What were you up to?"

"Who me?" she asks with an innocently raised eyebrow. "Well, I definitely was *not* upstairs. And my husband certainly did *not* bend me over a desk."

"Ahh, desk. Ross said you two were probably banging in a closet, but that didn't seem right," I tease.

"He what? Where is that little shit?" She stops and it's her turn to give me the critical once-over. "Why are you out in the foyer? You look like you're about to bolt any second." She glances at Rock. "Hi, Rock. Thank goodness you're here or she would've left by now."

Rock laughs, but doesn't respond to the observation. "We've been looking for you," he says instead.

"Here, let me take your coat, Hope. I'm sweating just looking at you."

"I think that's because—"

"Hello, Hope. Rock," Damon greets as he descends the

stairs. He stops behind Mara, curving an arm around her waist, looking completely calm and collected for a man who just nailed his wife over a desk—because *yes,* I totally believe that's exactly what they were doing upstairs.

"Come on, Hope. Hand over the coat," Mara says, holding out her hands.

Damon quirks an eyebrow at her and she shrugs. "I don't want her jetting out the door."

Behind me, Rock chuckles and helps me slip off my coat. Damon holds out his hands and takes it away.

"I can leave without it you know," I say, facing Mara. "Rock will keep me warm."

She rolls her eyes. "I'm sure he will. Now come on, I want to introduce you to the chair of the small firms committee."

Immediately suspicious, I stop in my tracks. "Why?"

"They need a co-chair."

"Oh, hell no. I don't want to do that." After my initial revulsion wears off, I think it over. "You know who would be good for it though? A friend of mine, Charlotte Clark."

"Is she here tonight?"

"No, but I'll mention it to her."

"I still want to introduce you."

"Fine." I throw Rock one last pleading look, but he stands there, spreads his hands and shrugs, as if there's nothing he can possibly do to save me from my determined friend.

CHAPTER THREE

Heidi

"Are you excited for your first tree, Alexa?" Charlotte asks, holding Alexa up and wiggling her from side to side.

"Tweee!" Alexa yells. We took her to the lights in the park show the other night and she's been yelling about trees, deer, and lights ever since. I can't wait to see how she reacts when we get the tree in the house and all lit up.

"Are you and Marcel going to the party tonight?" I ask.

"I'm not sure yet."

"Will your uncle be there?"

"As far as I know, he's on the road." She settles Alexa in her lap and hands her a plushy unicorn. "Are you upset you're not going?"

Do I like being included in club events? Yes. Do I *want* to hang out at Crystal Ball all night wondering which bunny or stripper has banged my fiancé in the past? Not so much.

"I'm fine with skipping it. I just don't want Murphy annoyed about missing it."

Charlotte casts a *you're-being-ridiculous* look my way. She nods to the window. "Have you seen him? He's more interested in decorating that tree tonight than anything else."

My mouth quirks. Murphy's as excited about this as I am. I can't deny it. "I haven't had a real tree since I lived with my grandmother. She hated Christmas, but Marcel would sneak a tree in the house when she was at church or something."

"Marcel was horrified when I told him I wanted one of those artificial pre-lit trees. He claims the pine scent will be worth the mess of needles all over the house."

"That sounds like my brother."

Once the guys finish with the dangerous machinery, we join them outside again. Alexa bursts into tears at the sight of the mutilated trees. "Nooo. Tweee," she cries, reaching her little mitten-covered hands toward the branches.

"It's okay. The trees are coming home with us."

At the word "home" she whips around. "Bed," she states.

"Are you tired?"

She shakes her head *no*. But these days she answers *no* to, well, almost everything. She'll be out cold before we hit the highway.

Blake and Marcel load the trees into the back of the

truck, securing them with rope while I buckle Alexa into her car seat.

"I bought a few strands of lights, but don't own enough ornaments for that monster," I say once we're on the road.

"Are you planning to decorate your tree in a particular theme?" Charlotte asks.

"Her *theme* when she was little was shove-as-much-tinsel-as-possible on the tree," Marcel answers.

"No one asked you." I flick his shoulder. "No tinsel for our tree. It's not baby-safe."

"I always wanted a hot-pink tree," Charlotte says. "Pink lights, ornaments, garland. Monochromatic pink."

I can't help laughing, because Charlotte has never struck me as a woman who yearns for a pink Christmas tree.

"Pink's not very Christmas-y," Blake says.

Her mouth twitches and I'm not sure if she's upset or something else.

"Well," I say, patting Marcel's shoulder. "The house is certainly big enough for more than one tree."

"No fake trees," he grumbles.

Blake reaches back and runs his hand up the back of my calf. "Alexa asleep?"

"Yup."

When Marcel had said earlier that he had *one stop* to make, I never suspected he meant a storage facility. And I didn't realize he still had boxes and furniture from our grandmother's house and from his old apartment.

Charlotte offers to stay in the car with Alexa, so I can help Marcel.

"Why do you still have all this stuff?"

He shrugs. "I got rid of most of it, but there were a few things I thought you might want once you had your own place." He rearranges boxes until he finds what he wants. "Plus, I've been saving these for you."

I recognize the battered cardboard box he offers me right away. "Mom's Christmas ornaments?"

"A few might be broken, so be careful opening them around Alexa."

"You don't want any of them?"

"No, they should be yours."

Searching through this box of ornaments with my mother is one of the few happy memories I have of her. "Thank you, Marcel."

"Is there anything else you want?"

I glance around the small space. "My old bedroom set and desk for Alexa? By the time we finally move into the house she'll probably be able to use it."

"Done. Murphy said he'd help me clear it out this week. I'll store the stuff at my place." He slings an arm around my shoulder and pulls me closer, dropping a kiss on my forehead. "I'm so glad you're here this year."

"Me too."

CHAPTER FOUR

WRATH

SHE HASN'T COME OUT AND SAID SO, BUT TRINITY'S NERVOUS about the club's Christmas party tonight. Maybe she's not even aware of it. But I know my wife. She hasn't stopped moving or working all day long and she's been unusually quiet.

First, she was up early baking cookies. Enough cookies to fill every flat surface in our kitchen.

Then she sat down to check emails, which led to her scrolling through photo galleries and retouching pictures from a recent shoot.

"Angel," I say, coming up behind her. "Trinity Studio is closed until after New Year's."

Without turning around, she shuts down her computer.

"You're right," she says, standing and facing me. She still seems jittery.

Luckily, I have something in mind to calm her down.

A dirty, perverted fantasy I've been waiting to fulfill for a while now.

She takes a step closer, curling her hands over my shoulders, and sliding her fingers against the base of my neck. "Are you feeling neglected?" she asks with a teasing pout.

That actually hadn't crossed my mind.

"What are you wearing to the party tonight?"

"Well, jeans if we're riding. I'll bring my dress and change there. It's a stretchy velvet material that shouldn't wrinkle too bad."

"Are you wearing stockings?"

She narrows her eyes. "Why are you so concerned about my fashion choices all of a sudden?"

I close my eyes. "I'm trying to get a visual."

Laughter, soft and sweet flows out of her and she pokes me in the chest. "You'll see later."

"I have a present for you."

"It's not Christmas yet."

"I've never been good at waiting."

"Wait." She gives me a skeptical squint. "Is it a present for *you* or me?"

"Both of us."

A spark of interest flares in her eyes. "Really?"

I raise an eyebrow in a silent challenge and she holds out her hand and I guide her into the bedroom.

Stalking over to my nightstand, I pull out the square

package. I ordered this a couple days ago and since it came early, I figured it was a sign that I should use it on her tonight.

I hand it to her and she laughs. "Remote controlled panty vibrator." Her honey eyes stare up at me, sparkling with amusement. "When did you turn into such a sadistic bastard?"

"You bring out the best in me."

She fists one of her hands in my shirt, pulling me down for a kiss. "What's your game plan? You want me in the kitchen wearing this, an apron, and nothing else?"

Hadn't thought of that, but now that she mentioned it, it's going on my list.

"Yeah, we'll definitely try that. But no, I thought you'd wear it for me tonight."

She raises an eyebrow. "Tonight? At the party?"

My reasoning seemed sound in my head. It would keep her attention on me instead of worrying about anything else.

"I'm not going to embarrass you in front of anyone. The whole point is no one knows but us."

She cocks her head and stares at me for a second. "Just how much porn do you watch when I'm at the studio?"

"Angel, I don't *need* porn." I tap the side of my head. "We have years and years ahead of us before I run out of filthy things I want to do with you. *Years*."

I MUST BE out of my damn mind to agree to this. But dammit, I have a hard time saying *no* to anything Wyatt wants. Anything. Even this. Which seems like a really bad idea.

But also insanely hot.

"I should have you wear this whenever we're not together. That way you'd know how often I think about you."

I reach up and loop my arms around his neck. "Somehow you're the best combination of sweet and dirty a woman could ask for."

"Thank you."

He hooks his fingers in my jeans and flips the button loose. Our eyes meet as he slowly works them down my hips.

"Rules are," he says in a low seductive voice that has the power to lull me into doing whatever he asks. "I'll give you a buzz here and there. But you can't *come* unless you're with me."

"A buzz here and there won't be enough anyway. I'll probably look like I'm having a seizure."

He ducks his head and laughs while I kick my jeans to the side.

"More than a buzz."

"That's mean. What if you work me up so much that I

can't come at all?" I squeeze my thighs together just thinking about the unbearable frustration.

He leans down and nips my earlobe. "Then I promise to suck on your little clit until you explode."

A full body shiver of excitement runs through me. "Uff," I grunt. Great. Now my brain won't function.

"Let's play with it at home before we leave." His lips quirk. "Just to get the hang of it."

"Sure. We wouldn't want it to malfunction at the party."

"Right," he says, ignoring my sarcasm.

He strips off my shirt and pushes me back on the bed. "Put your feet up," he says, patting the mattress on either side of me.

When I don't put my feet quite as far apart as he wants, he wastes no time spreading me wider.

His big warm hands tug my underwear down my legs. "Soaked," he murmurs. "You're more interested than you're letting on."

He kneels in front of me, putting his face almost directly in my pussy. His big, rough hands run up and down my legs, soothing and relaxing me.

"I don't think anyone would believe the big bad Wrath gets on his knees for me."

He flicks his gaze up my body, a hint of a smile playing at the corners of his mouth. "You're my queen. I'll always bow to you." He seals that promise with a feathery kiss against the inside of my ankle, then brushes his lips over the other foot. "Only you."

My eyes burn from the sweet reverence in his voice. I

reach down and capture one of his hands. "I love you, Wyatt."

"Love you too, Angel."

A hint of wickedness enters his voice. "Now, let's test this out."

He holds up the panty contraption and I pick up my feet for him to slip it on. "Lift up," he says when he reaches my hips.

I'm panting with anticipation and excitement by the time he has it placed the way he wants. He holds up small black square with a clicker-type button in the center. "Tonight, I'll use this. But I can also program it from my phone."

"Goody."

My sass is rewarded with a flick of a button.

"Oh, shit!" Once the initial shock wears off, I realize the vibration isn't even that strong. More of a pleasant humming.

"How's that?" he asks, running his hands over my legs and hips.

"Nice."

"Just nice? Hmm." He flicks the button up another notch.

"Good."

Another level.

"Oh! Okay. Whoa. That's more intense."

He grunts in satisfaction and sets it at the highest level.

My hips shoot up and I let out a sharp scream. "Holy fuck."

"Strong little thing, right?" he asks with an evil laugh. Christ, he's dangerous with a new toy.

"Fuck. Yes."

He slips his hand between my legs, pressing the little unit tight against me and I fucking lose it. "Fuck, Wyatt."

Jealous of the little toy or impatient—I can't tell which—he shoves it aside and buries his face against me, eagerly sucking and licking.

Overwhelmed, I bury my hands in his hair, pulling harder than I mean to. He growls a warning against me, but I'm way too far gone, screaming and bucking against his face.

Then his mouth is gone and the vibrator returns.

"Need to fuck you," he grinds out.

I blink and he's tearing off his clothes, shoving his jeans down, but too frantic to take them all the way off. I'd help, but I can't move.

He falls on the bed next to me. "Up."

When I don't move fast enough, he sits up and pulls me on top of him. I fumble with the panty thing and he brushes my hands away. "Leave it. My cock needs to snuggle up with your pussy. Now."

I'm embarrassingly slippery and easily slide down, groaning the whole time.

"Good. Fuck. So good, Angel."

His hands clamp down on my hips and he moves me the way he needs. Up and down, back and forth. I'm a happy, blissful ragdoll in his grasp.

He comes with a roar a few minutes later and pulls me down, hugging me to his chest. After a couple seconds, he kisses the top of my head.

"I think level four is for home-use only," he teases.

He pats the mattress until he finds the remote and shuts it off.

"Oh, thank God. I don't think I can take anymore."

"Well, you better rest up, because you're definitely wearing that tonight."

I run my teeth over his nipple and he groans. "Stop."

Another little nip has him flicking the panties back on.

And that's how we spend the rest of our afternoon. Teasing and tormenting each other into unconsciousness.

CHAPTER FIVE

ROCK

"Did our wives take off?" Damon asks as he returns from the coat check.

I tilt my head toward the main room the party's being held in. "Mara seemed very determined to introduce Hope to some people."

"She's invested in having more female attorneys in leadership positions." The corners of his mouth twitch in a way that says he's proud of whatever it is Mara's working toward. "She'll have Hope volunteering for a dozen committees before you leave."

Somehow I doubt that. As sweet as my wife is, she rarely gets talked into doing anything she doesn't want to do. "I hear you're running for State Senate."

"I am. Figured I could do some good there."

"I don't doubt it. If I can help out, let me know."

His expression freezes and I almost laugh at his discomfort. "I'm not offering to break any kneecaps for you, Damon. Just a regular campaign donation."

Like a good politician he smooths over the awkwardness with a bland smile. "Of course. Thank you. That's very generous."

We stop at the bar before searching for the girls. Unsurprisingly, my friend Tony is there and he gives me an enthusiastic handshake. We speak for a few minutes. Mostly pleasantries about his family. I spot Glassman, the attorney who handles the club's legal work across the room and he nods at me. If he's surprised to see me here, it doesn't show.

Hope and Mara are standing in a small circle of people. Damon and I head their way. I quietly walk up behind Hope and slip my arm around her waist.

She turns to give me a hint of a smile and accepts the small glass of ginger ale I hand her. "Thank you."

When there's a break in the conversation, Hope introduces me to her colleagues. They're far more interested in talking to Damon, and I'm not insulted. Damon manages to smoothly transition the conversation back to his wife.

Hope tips her glass back, taking a sip of her soda, and flashes three fingers at me.

Chuckling at the subtle signal, I excuse us.

Hope gives Mara a triumphant smile and waves at her over her shoulder.

"Are you sure you want to leave so early? We still have time before the party at CB starts."

"I'm sure," she answers without a trace of doubt in her voice.

At the edge of the room, Glassman stops us. "Rock, good to see you." He turns to Hope and holds out his hand. "Ms. Kendall, I don't usually see you at these events."

"I try to avoid them as much as possible," she answers with an awkward laugh. If there's one thing I love about my wife, she's unflinchingly honest. Even when I know she doesn't mean to be. "My friend, Mara, is on the board."

"Ah, Judge Oak's wife. I see," he says as if that makes it all click into place for him.

I don't care for the condescending tone Glassman uses with my wife. Is this how he would normally speak to her? Or does he think I'll be impressed?

"And I spoke to Angie. They need a co-chair for the small firms committee," Hope adds, surprising me.

"Uh, oh. Better stop her now, Rock. She'll be dragging you to more of these events if you let her do that."

Let her do that? My fists curl, but punching Glassman isn't the solution in this situation. Instead, I pull my face into a mask of confusion, cock my head, and use my own condescending tone. "Care to explain your reasoning?"

Glassman clearly didn't expect a question like that out of me. He opens his mouth, sputters, seems to realize how rude his comment actually was, and shakes his head. "They'll be lucky to have you, Ms. Kendall," he finally says.

"Well, we were just heading out. Good to see you again," Hope says, taking my hand.

We make it three steps closer to the door when Mara calls out, stopping us.

"You sneaky wench. You're leaving already?" she asks, hugging Hope to her chest. "Thank you so much for coming." She glances up at me. "Both of you."

Damon joins us and walks Hope to the coat closet. I'm so focused on my wife's backside that when Mara stops, I almost knock her over.

Unfazed, she turns and presses one hand to my arm. "Thank you, Rock."

"For?"

"For being so good to her. Not getting in her way. Making her stronger. Take your pick."

Not sure what to say, I stand there, waiting for her to elaborate.

Her lips curl into a teasing smirk. "I know you're used to being *the king* in your world, but here you step back and quietly support her without trying to dominate the conversation." She flicks her wrist toward the party. "You don't try to make it all about you."

"I'm not a lawyer."

She tilts her head in a way that says *don't be dense*. "You know what I mean."

"I think I do."

"Good." She walks me to the door where we meet up with Damon and Hope.

Once we're outside, Hope sucks in a deep breath and immediately starts coughing as the cold air shocks her lungs.

"Careful, Baby Doll," I murmur, patting her back.

"What were you and Mara talking about?" she asks as we walk up the street.

I'm not sure what to make of Mara's assessment of me yet. "She just thanked me for coming."

While my brief talk with Mara was nice, I'm still pissed about the conversation with Glassman. Once we're in the car, I decide to ask her about it. "Is Glassman always that… dismissive when he talks to you?"

"Uh, yeah." She snorts. "It's not like he's the only one. A lot of male attorneys can't help themselves. He's more polite than most."

"Maybe the club needs a new law firm," I mutter.

"Don't you dare. He's an excellent attorney. Besides, your response was beautiful. It might have helped him realize he sounded like a sexist ass."

"I doubt it." I put the truck in drive and steer us toward the highway. "Damon doesn't seem to be like that."

"He's not. Don't get me wrong. He's a terrifying judge to argue in front of. Low tolerance for pontificating and wasting his time. But he's equally hard on the male attorneys, has never asked me when I plan to start a family, and doesn't suggest I'd appear more "professional" in a skirt suit when I wear pants to court."

"Jesus Christ, seriously? Who's said that shit to you?"

"Are you going to beat them up for me?" she taunts.

"Maybe. Now I feel shitty I'm taking you to a strip club."

She lets out a huff of laughter. "Why? At least it's honest.

"Glassman aside, are you happy you went?"

"Yes and thank you for coming. I felt better having you with me."

"I always have your back, baby."

"I know you do," she answers quietly.

"And now you get to do the same for me."

She reaches over and slides her hand up my leg, resting it on my thigh, distracting the hell out of me.

"It's not quite the same," she says. "You're the *president*. Everyone respects you no matter what. And you're always calm and controlled in every situation."

I prefer her version to the truth. Which is, "Most of the time I bite my tongue more than I want to."

"Oh, I know you do," she teases. "I can tell by the tight smile that forms right here." She traces her fingertip over my cheek, down to the corner of my mouth. "And the muscles in your neck tense up." Her finger moves lower, blazing a path over my skin.

"Are you trying to get us into an accident?"

I glance over long enough to catch her batting her eyelashes in an innocent *who me* expression.

"I'm just trying to explain that I want to help make things *less tense* for you tonight."

"I have some suggestions."

"I'm sure you do." Her hand drops from my neck to my lap and slides over my crotch, squeezing enough to scramble my brain.

"Jesus, woman. Control yourself."

She takes her hand away and sits back.

"I didn't say don't touch me at all."

"No, you're right. I can't control myself."

At the next stoplight, I reach over and settle my hand on her knee. "Spread your legs for me."

"No."

"No?"

"Not yet."

Hope teasing and challenging me—there's nothing I love more. I'm tempted to keep driving just to continue our conversation. I attempt to slide my hand under her dress again. "What does that mean?"

She giggles and pushes my hand away. "The light's green."

CHAPTER SIX

Heidi

As we make the turn into Marcel's driveway, he glances in the rearview mirror. "Alexa awake yet?"

Maybe she heard her name or she knew we were almost at the house, but she suddenly yelps and reaches for the window, smudging her little fingers against the glass.

"I think so." I finally look out the window to see what has her attention. "Marcel, what's this?"

Next to me, Charlotte squeals and claps her hands together. "Alexa seemed to love the lights in the park so much, Marcel wanted to create his own version for her."

All the trees on either side of the driveway are decorated with multiple strands of vibrant Christmas lights. Some trees even have twinkling white snowflakes dangling from the lower branches.

My eyes burn and for a few seconds I can't swallow over the lump in my throat. "This must have taken you forever."

"Murphy helped me early this morning and Carter finished while we were getting the trees," Marcel explains.

"That's where you were this morning?" I ask Blake.

He turns and winks. "Where else?"

"You didn't notice in the daytime." Marcel grins. "That's why I wanted to keep us out until dark. I was hoping she'd wake up in time."

Alexa's excited babbles climb higher in pitch as we roll closer to the house.

To the left, a couple families of glowing white reindeer are tastefully grazing in the yard. On the right side of the house there's a giant—and I mean *huge*—red, and white motorcycle, a jolly snowman, and even little puppies frolicking. The combined glow of the decorations is enough to light up the front yard. Some of the lawn ornaments are animated and Alexa doesn't seem to know where to look first.

My brother pulls the truck to the side of the driveway and turns it off while I zip Alexa into her coat and wrestle her into her mittens.

Charlotte's door opens and Carter's red-cheeked face peers inside. "I just finished! I'm *so* glad you guys didn't get here like fifteen minutes sooner. That Santa was a bitch. He had me cursing up a storm," he says in excited rush.

"Everything looks great. Thanks, Carter," Marcel says.

Charlotte jumps down and hugs her brother, while Blake

opens my door and takes Alexa for me. I climb out and offer to hold her, but he grabs my hand instead. Alexa stretches her little arms toward the lights over her head, frustrated she can't quite reach.

"No. No touch. Ouch," I warn her and she quickly pulls her arms against her chest and keeps them there.

Marcel tickles his finger over her cheek and she jerks her head around laughing when she sees it's him. "You listen so much better than your mom did. I told her *no* and she'd try to stick the lights in her mouth."

"Don't give Alexa ideas," Blake says.

"I used to worry she was going to get electrocuted like the cat in *Christmas Vacation*," Marcel teases.

"Shut up. I did not," I protest. Although, it does sound like something I would've done. Maybe.

"You did all the critters by yourself, Carter?" Blake asks.

"Yeah, it wasn't hard. Teller already had them ready to go out in the garage. I just needed to place 'em and plug 'em in." He points to the house. "I ran out of time to do the porch railings or anything else."

"We'll do them tomorrow. Thanks, Carter," Marcel says, pulling him in for a one-armed hug. Carter ducks his head and mumbles, "You're welcome."

We spend the next hour or so wandering up and down the driveway, checking out all the decorations. Alexa's enchanted by everything.

I walk up and brush my shoulder against Marcel. "Thank you."

He holds out his arms to take Alexa and kisses her cheeks. "You like the lights, baby?"

She giggles and claps her mittens together. "Thnow!" she says, pointing at the glittering white ornaments hanging from one of the trees.

"That's right," I say. "Maybe we'll have a White Christmas this year."

Alexa's not sure what to think about that. She squirms, searching for Blake and stretches her little arms trying to get to him.

"Oh, I see how it is," Marcel laughs, handing her over. He slings his arm around me and pulls me closer. "I always wanted to do this when you were little, but we either didn't have the money or Gram would've had a fit."

I tip my head back to take him in and my heart squeezes at the happy expression on his face. "You're the best big brother. And an even better uncle."

MURPHY

TELLER AND HEIDI seem to be having a moment, so I carry Alexa a few feet away to show her more of the decorations. Her big eyes and awed smile totally make up for my lack of sleep this morning. She wants to see everything and with my assistance even takes a few tentative steps to "pet" the deer. It's chilly and she burrows against my chest, eventually falling asleep mumbling about "twees" and "dee-dees."

Heidi's almost as entranced by the decorations as Alexa and I can't wait to show her what's waiting at home.

"You guys staying for dinner?" Marcel asks a few minutes later.

"Nothing fancy," Charlotte says. "Make your own pizzas. I have fresh dough and all the toppings."

"That sounds awesome." Heidi rubs her hands together. "I'm starving, even though all I did was sit in the truck and watch you two cut down the trees."

"Murphy and I are going to unload the trees, but we'll be right in."

I hand Alexa over to Heidi and she thankfully doesn't wake up.

"You want me to help?" Carter asks.

"Nah, we got this," Teller says. "Go help Charlotte."

Carter narrows his eyes but follows the girls inside.

"He okay with you bossing him around all the time?" I ask.

Teller stops and cocks his head as if the thought never occurred to him. "I don't boss him around."

"Sure, okay."

He frowns and then seems to shake it off. "Can we get the trees taken care of before you lecture me on how to manage my family?" Teller says, dropping the tailgate of his truck.

"Didn't realize it was such a touchy subject."

"Just grab your end of the tree, smart ass."

We toss mine in the back of my pickup first. I help him carry the other one up the porch stairs.

"Do you even remember which one was which?" he asks as we navigate the steps.

"Not really. Does it matter?"

"Heidi seemed set on one." He ducks his head and laughs. "I just can't remember *which* one."

"It's not like she won't see both."

He drops his smile and sets his end of the tree down. "Speaking of, Charlotte meant it earlier, we'd like to have you guys stay Christmas Eve if you want. It'd be nice to wake up and open presents and stuff together." He shrugs as if he's worried I'm going to make fun of his suggestion. "See Alexa open her stuff."

"It's your first Christmas in your new house. Sure you want us crashing it?"

"You know I do and Charlotte wouldn't have asked if she didn't mean it."

"I'll talk to Heidi."

Only because I've known Marcel so long, can I tell he's not satisfied with my answer. But he's been working hard on staying out of my relationship with Heidi and doesn't persist.

"We bringing in this tree or not?" I ask.

He glances behind him. "Can you keep Charlotte busy in the kitchen?"

"Isn't that your job?"

Instead of laughing, he frowns. "I'm serious. I have a surprise I want to set up for her upstairs."

"If it's a sex swing, make sure you anchor it into one of the—"

"It's not a sex swing, you dick. And what…never mind. Just keep her downstairs."

"Let's get inside first."

Charlotte already has a place ready in the living room

for the tree and after we secure it in the stand, Teller ghosts out.

Slinging an arm around Charlotte's shoulders, I steer her toward the kitchen. "What was that you said about make-your-own pizzas?"

"Where'd Marcel go?"

"Bathroom. He'll probably be awhile."

What? Marcel didn't say exactly *how* I was supposed to keep her downstairs.

CHAPTER SEVEN

Charlotte

WE'RE FINISHING DINNER WHEN CARTER'S PHONE RINGS AND he answers it at the table.

"It's Bianca," he explains before getting up and walking away.

"Oooo!" Murphy and Teller heckle and make kissy-noises at Carter until he runs from the room.

"Really?" Heidi says, throwing her stern-mom look at both of them. She swings her gaze my way. "Is Bianca his girlfriend?"

"I can't keep track of what they are."

Carter ends up leaving to pick Bianca up from somewhere. Murphy and Heidi duck out a few minutes later.

Then Marcel and I are finally alone.

He reaches out and draws me into his arms.

"Did you have a good day?" I ask.

"The best. Thank you."

"You did all the work."

He answers with a happy humming sound and squeezes me tighter. "Want to finish decorating the tree?"

"You really don't want to go to the party?" I ask. "I bought a tiny dress and everything." I'm not particularly eager to attend the club's holiday party being held at the strip club they own. I'm looking forward to the more family-friendly events at the clubhouse over the next two weeks.

I also recognize, that as Teller's ol' lady I'm expected to attend events like this and I don't want him to think he has to skip something to please me.

He pulls back and raises an eyebrow. "So about this slinky dress."

"Who said it was slinky?"

"Tiny. Whatever. Where is it?"

"In my closet."

"Go put it on for me."

"Are we going?"

Instead of answering, he pulls back and stares at me with one cocky eyebrow raised.

Challenging me.

"Do you want me to give you a lap dance too?" I ask.

"Maybe."

I skip up the stairs, already picturing sliding on the dress and twisting and teasing him in time to some sexy music.

There's an unfamiliar pinkish glow coming from our bedroom and I stop dead when I cross the threshold.

The pinkest, most perfect Christmas tree stands in our room, framed by the picture window that faces our backyard. My jaw drops and I blink a few times.

I sense, more than hear, Marcel enter the room behind me. His hands land on my hips and he molds himself against my back. He leans in and brushes a kiss on my cheek. "Do you like it?" he asks in a low voice.

Words. For a few seconds I can't come up with any. "I really do. You must think I'm an idiot, but I always wanted…" I huff out a breath. "Thank you."

"I didn't have time to do more than unpack it and plug it in." He gestures to a few bags on the floor next to the tree. "I bought some decorations—all pink—but we can—"

"It's perfect." I glance at the tree again, my vision swimming. "You didn't have to get such a big tree. I only meant a little tabletop one."

"Nope. My girl wants a hot-pink Christmas tree, she's going to have the biggest one I can find."

"We don't have to keep it in the bedroom. Unless you don't—"

"Sunshine, I'm more than man enough to have a pink tree any place I want in my house." He grips my chin, forcing me to look at him. "I put it in our bedroom so you can wake up every morning and remember there's *nothing* your man won't do to make you happy."

Every day we've been together he makes me fall more and more in love with him.

Sliding my arms around his neck, I reach up and kiss along his jaw. "Are you ready for your lap dance?"

"Can I see your dress?" he counters.

"I thought the purpose of the lap dance was for my clothes to come *off*."

"Go put it on for me."

I nudge and push him into the big, comfy armchair in the corner of our bedroom. Right next to the tree.

He falls into the chair with a hint of a smile playing on his lips. Leaning over, I push his legs apart and lean down. "Wait here like a good boy."

He twists his lips into a smirk and sits back.

Slowly backing away, I make my way to the closet and take out the dress. Changing right in front of him isn't exactly sexy, so I take it into the bathroom and close the door.

Soft music fills the bedroom and my stomach flutters with anticipation.

I really did buy this dress with the party in mind. Where else do I have to wear a short, skin-tight velvet dress with cut-outs at the sides and midriff? It's a deep, rich wine color and has three-quarter sleeves to balance all the exposed skin in the middle. I planned to wear it with lacy stockings and knee-high boots, but for now, I leave my feet bare. I pull my hair into a messy knot on the top of my head and dab on a dark wine-red lipstick that drives Marcel nuts every time I wear it.

Before opening the door, I flick the bathroom light off.

Marcel's still sitting in the chair and he focuses all of his attention on me standing in the doorway.

With one hand, he beckons me closer. "Come show me."

While my body yearns to rush over the second he asks, I take my time, enjoying the weight of his appreciative gaze.

"Stunning," he murmurs.

Not the "hot" I expected. Even better.

When I'm about five feet away, I slow my movements, stopping to pose and touch myself as if that's all I plan to do.

"Closer," he demands. "I want to touch."

"No touching."

He lets out a rumbling chuckle. "We'll see."

I move closer, my steps and movements following the rhythm of the music he chose. When I'm within grabbing distance, he sits forward and fits his hands around my waist, pulling me between his legs. "You're so pretty. I have to take you out."

"Do you want your dance first?" I ask, turning in his hold and arching my back, shaking my butt in his face. His hands slide the material of my dress up to my hips and he sinks his teeth into one ass cheek, biting only enough to tease.

I push the dress into place as a song with a quicker, sensual beat plays. Slowly, I turn, working my hips in time with the melody, trailing my fingertips up my sides and under my breasts.

"Nice," he says, sitting back.

On the next slide down, I gather the dress in my hands and drag it up and over my head.

TELLER

Everything Charlotte does turns me on.

Walks into the room?

Done.

At the stove making dinner?

We've burned a few meals when I couldn't wait to have her.

But this? Playfully dancing for me. The barely there thong. The dark red dress. The lipstick. That fucking lipstick—it's called blood moon or unicorn blood, something silly with blood in the name, which is appropriate because every time she wears it, all my blood rushes to my cock.

While she twists and turns in front of me, I run my big, rough hands up her smooth bare thighs, settling at her waist to turn her around. Again, I slide my hands over her hips, her ass and down her legs. She's all silky skin and thin strips of black lace.

Hooking my thumbs in the straps of her thong, I slide it down her legs and throw it toward the bed. "You'll wear that for me later."

"Okay," she whispers. Her knees weaken and I grip her tighter, pulling her to me and resting my forehead against her stomach. Her fingers run through my hair and down my back. She's still gently swaying her hips to the music and I smile against her skin.

With her fingers on my shoulders, she pushes me back. "Take your cock out."

"Take your bra off."

"This isn't a negotiation."

Charlotte knows *exactly* who she's playing with and *how* to play me. The more she tries ordering me around, the harder I'm going to fuck her.

I ease back in the chair and slowly unbuckle my belt. Giving her as good a show as she's given me. Balancing her hands on my legs, she lowers herself to the floor—not usually where I like her, but I'm letting her run the show—for now. I'm so hard, my cock springs free and she wastes no time wrapping her hand around me. Love her touch—gentle but possessive as hell. I groan and sit back as her other hand works open my jeans even more. She slides her hand inside, cradling my balls with the perfect amount of pressure.

"Good?" she asks.

"Fuck yes," I manage to answer even though my voice is tight from wanting her.

Her hand strokes in a lazy way—loose and slow.

A low moan of agonized pleasure rumbles out of me the second her lips close over my cock. "Fuck. All the way. I want that lipstick decorating my cock when you're done."

"Mmm," she hums, the sound vibrating through me.

Stars gather at the edges of my vision as she takes me all the way down and sucks her way back. "Fuck," I breathe out.

Every muscle in my body clenches hard but I'm not ready to rush to the finish. I touch the back of her head and she moans a little louder. My other hand settles on her shoulder.

The desire to have every part of her seeps into me. Without thinking, I wrap my hand around her ponytail and tug her off.

Her tongue darts out, licking her bottom lip. Dark red rings my cock, and her lipstick's smeared. I reach out and wipe her cheek with my thumb. "Good job."

"Why'd you stop me?"

Words can't explain it, so I cradle her face with my hands and kiss her. When that's not enough, I pull her up, lifting her and carrying her to the bed where we roll onto the soft blankets together. I have to touch her everywhere. She sits up for me to work her bra off and then I'm filling my hands with her full breasts. Her tongue slides against mine while her fingers tease my shirt up over my head. I sit up and toss my shirt and push my jeans the rest of the way off. Then I'm back on top of her pressing rough kisses to her mouth, nipping at her neck. "I love you," I mumble, tasting more of her skin.

She places her hands on my cheeks, urging me to look in her eyes. "I love you too." Her tone is serious, but there's a frisky gleam in her eyes. "But don't let that stop you from fucking me hard."

With that, she rolls over and attempts to wriggle away.

Crawling over her, I pin her down with my thighs and bodyweight. "Where do you think you're going?" I growl against her neck.

She buries her face in the comforter to muffle her

laughter. Her hips wiggle and she tries to raise her ass. Normally, I'd make her wait, draw this out, but I can't.

"Spread those legs, bad girl."

She fists her hands in the comforter, dragging it toward us. Her hips shift and I slide the head of my cock against her and suck in a deep breath.

"Fuck, you feel good."

She sighs and arches her back. I wrap my arm around her waist, yanking her to me and push inside her with one, long rough shove.

I wrap my hand in her hair, pulling her head up. No more hiding and teasing. She shrieks and braces herself on her elbows, pushing back against me. "More."

"You want more?" I ask, taunting her with a gentle stroke. "More what?"

"Harder."

I pull back, almost all the way, then push inside a little faster. "Like that?"

Tired of my teasing, she groans and raises up to hands and knees, working herself back and forth on my cock. My fingers slip through her hair, pulling the elastic free, so it's wild and messy.

I clasp her hips, stopping her movements and pull out, flipping her over. She blinks up at me, but doesn't protest. Then I'm covering her with my body. She's slick and soft and so damn hot when I sink inside her. "You want it rough tonight, Sunshine."

It's a statement, not a question and I punctuate it with a wicked roll of my hips. Her teeth tug at her bottom lip and she nods.

Our eyes lock and the connection ratchets up my pleasure to a whole new level.

Gently, I press my thumb and fingers against the pulse points at the sides of her neck. My quick, furious thrusts slow as I watch every flutter of her lashes. "Oh, oh, oh," she gasps, her body writhing under me.

Only when she's on the brink do I let go. She comes so hard, back arching, lips parted, relentless cries of pleasure.

Done. My skin sizzles and a jolt of heat rocks down my spine. "Coming," I warn and she murmurs encouragement. I curse one last time before shooting hard inside her.

In our bed. Surrounded by the glow from our pink tree.

CHAPTER EIGHT

Heidi

After dinner, Blake assures my brother we can handle getting our tree to Rock and Hope's house on our own.

I fling my arms around Marcel for a big hug. "Thank you so much for everything."

He squeezes me back just as hard. "You bet, kid."

Everyone ends up walking outside with us and thankfully, Alexa had fallen asleep again after dinner or she'd probably have a hissy fit when we leave all the lights behind.

"I can't believe you guys did all that," I say as we glide down the driveway. I'm still in awe of all the work my brother put into the decorations.

Murphy glances over. "He wanted to surprise you."

"Well, he did." I think over how much has changed in the last few months and my heart's ready to burst. "I'm so happy he's happy. He has his own place and just seems so…at peace. Charlotte's good for him."

"She is," he agrees.

"I bet some of the guys think he's moving too fast, but I'm glad he didn't screw around. I hope they set a date soon."

"*You* haven't set a date yet."

"That's different," I say, staring out the window.

"Hey." Blake reaches over and rubs my leg. "What're you thinking about?"

"Our wedding. Let's get married next summer. After graduation."

He glances over and raises an eyebrow. "Yeah? Are you sure you're on schedule to finish next May?"

"Pretty sure." I glance in the backseat and reach out to fix Alexa's blanket. "She should be big enough to be part of our wedding."

Blake catches my hand and pulls it to his mouth, kissing my open palm. "I like the sound of that," he says softly.

It's a short ride to the club's property and we're pulling in front of the clubhouse a few minutes later.

"I'm going to see if someone's around to help us with the tree," Blake says.

I clap my hand over my mouth. "Shoot. Everyone's probably at the party."

"Nah, someone's always around."

"Blake," I call out before he shuts his door. "I want to come inside with you."

Without answering, he unbuckles Alexa and picks her up. She fusses but settles once she's in his arms. "What do you need?" he asks as he meets me on the other side of the truck.

"I still have some boxes stored in Hope's closet upstairs. A few ornaments for the tree might be in there."

He hesitates for a second before answering. "Okay."

Inside, we run into Sparky and Stash on their way to the party at Crystal Ball. "We can help with that," Sparky says, running to the closet to grab a pair of gloves.

Blake hands me a key for upstairs. "Go ahead. I'll come meet you and carry over whatever you need when we're done."

"Thank you."

Alexa's fully awake now and I have to stop in the bathroom for a diaper change before heading upstairs. It's oddly quiet. Not a biker or bunny in sight. Rock and Hope's old room is stuffy when I enter, so I open a few windows, making a mental note to close them before I leave.

Now that she's clean and had some snooze time, Alexa's eager to explore the new space.

"You spent lots of time here when you were itty bitty," I tell her. She giggle-gurgles and continues her investigation.

Keeping an eye on her while I pull down the boxes I want isn't easy, but once I'm sitting on the floor, she makes her way back to me. Curious about what I'm up to.

Ignoring one box in particular, I pry open another that I think is most likely to contain the ornaments I'm after. I've bounced around to so many different places in the last few years, that I haven't seen some of these things in a while.

Some are unimportant papers from high school that I threw in the box, because I packed them in a hurry. I set those aside to toss in the trash later and Alexa grabs for them, flinging the pages in the air.

"Having fun making a mess?" I tease, scooping her up and settling her in my lap. "Look, Uncle Marcel made these when he was younger." I hold one of the four ornaments up watching the sparkles shift and twirl from the movement. The glitter-filled globes are clear plastic, so thankfully they're not in danger of breaking when Alexa bats at them with her little hands. They're the product of an after-school "young entrepreneur" program Marcel was part of during his high school days. The class made and sold these ornaments, but Marcel said he saved the best ones for me and I've always kept them in a special place, hoping to have my own tree to put them on one day.

"Twee!" Alexa yells.

"Yup, we're going to put these on our tree."

The door opens, light from the hallway spilling into the room. "Find what you wanted?" Blake asks, leaving the door open.

I hold one of the ornaments out to him and he smiles. "I remember those."

"Da, da, da," Alexa screeches, reaching for Blake.

"Are you helping mommy or making a mess?" he asks, scooping her up and nodding at the papers.

Alexa glances down. "Mess."

"Well, at least she's honest," I joke.

Blake eyes the boxes in front of me. "Are these all coming back with us tonight?"

"No. Just this one. We don't have a lot of space right now. The others can wait until we move into our house."

His gaze roams to the box I pushed to the side earlier.

"There's nothing Christmas-y in that one," I say, stopping Blake from asking about the most embarrassing one of all.

A guilty twist to his mouth gives me pause.

"What?" I ask.

"Nothing. Are you sure you don't want it?"

"I do, but I can't unpack it right now." And not just because we don't have our own place yet.

He's still staring at me and I can't take the scrutiny. I pick myself up from the floor and dust off my jeans. The box of ornaments goes on the shelf next to me so I don't forget to take them with us. And I start returning the others to the closet.

"Why are you looking at me like that?"

His gaze strays to the box again, then back to me.

The box that's full of years of memories with Blake. Figurines he gave me for my birthdays, ticket stubs, seashells, postcards, notes, all of it rests inside that brown cardboard. Younger Heidi kept every precious memory she could hold onto.

It finally occurs to me that I stored that box here a while ago. Back when Murphy still lived a few doors down and I was headed all the way in Alaska.

"Did you look through my stuff?" I ask quietly.

He meets my eyes and doesn't so much as flinch. "I missed you."

Tears burn and threaten to fall, but I take a deep breath,

willing them away. If he saw all of those things, he knows what a silly girl I was. But he should also know how much I've always loved him. "And?"

"I love you."

I take a step closer and he holds out his free arm, pulling me against him. Alexa waves her arms and squeals, touching both of our faces with her fingers.

Blake leans down and brushes a soft, warm kiss against my lips.

"Come on. Let's go see the tree." He ruffles Alexa's hair. "Want to put lights on the tree?"

"Twee!"

"I'll take that as a *yes*."

"No!"

I burst out laughing.

After the boxes are put away. I grab the ornaments and take Blake's free hand.

"It's so quiet with everyone out," I comment as we pass the closed doors to the brothers' rooms.

"Doesn't happen often."

Big, fat snowflakes are slowly drifting to the ground as we step outside. Alexa swats and grabs for them, then finally tries to catch the flakes on her tongue. I'm so consumed with watching her, I almost don't notice the path to Rock and Hope's house is alive with lights.

Not the normal ground lights that mark the trail through the woods. No, this is the glow of white lights wrapped around tree trunks, creating a magical tunnel. Alexa *ooos* and *ahhs,* reaching up and then yanking her hand back as if she remembers my warning from earlier.

"Blake, this is beautiful. When did you?" I have no doubt he's the one who lovingly wrapped strand after strand of tiny bulbs around each tree trunk.

"This morning." He cracks a smile. "Your brother stole *my* idea. It's not as much—"

"It's perfect. So pretty. Thank you."

He brushes the back of his hand over my cheek. "Anything to see you smile, beautiful."

CHAPTER NINE

ROCK

"I'M GLAD YOU'RE WITH ME TONIGHT," I SAY, SLIDING MY hand over Hope's.

"Why aren't we having the party up at the clubhouse this year?"

I sigh and consider how to explain. "We didn't only invite Lost Kings. We've got Wolf Knights—"

"Trying to repair that relationship after Teller stole their president's niece?" she jokes.

"Kind of." I huff out a laugh. "Except for some weirdness here and there, our clubs get along. The new president is the guy who was in business with Wrath. So no repairs needed."

"Wolf Knights were at our wedding. So they've been to the clubhouse."

"Right. Well, I have a couple members from the Devil's Demons coming too. You've met them before—at our wedding."

"I remember."

I saved the best for last. I still can't believe Z talked me into having Loco at a club party. But he's our biggest customer and we've been in business with his crew for a long damn time. He's more than proved his loyalty over the last two years. It was time. I also might have a business opportunity for him that will benefit both of us. "There's a local crew we do a lot of business with. Have for years. The guy who runs it will be here with a few of his crew." And some of the escorts who work for him, but I'll save that tidbit for Hope to discover on her own.

She seems to think that over. "I'm assuming this is the guy who takes custody of Sparky's babies when they're finished growing?"

I choke on my laughter but don't confirm or deny her guess.

"Sparky will be there too. He has some product to show off."

"Product my ass." Hope laughs. "He probably wants to see Willow."

"Oh, really?" I should've known there was a reason he'd been dragging his ass out of the basement more frequently lately.

"Sway's coming too, right?" she asks. There's a catch in her voice I don't care for. None of my brothers should ever make my wife nervous. Maybe Sway deserves a few more punches in the face. "Will Tawny be there too?"

"A party full of strippers and bunnies? No, Tawny won't be joining him."

"Gross," she mutters.

I shrug. It is what it is. Sway's marital problems aren't my concern.

"Everyone will know who you are because you'll be wearing your patch. Murphy's not coming, but Z, Wrath, Dex, Ravage, Hoot, and Birch will all be here. Teller's supposed to stop by later. So there'll be plenty of familiar faces."

"As long as I have Trinity to hang with, I'll be fine."

I pull into the back parking lot at Crystal Ball and find a spot away from the door and any other vehicles. Hope twists and reaches for something on the back seat.

"What are you looking for?"

"Your bag. I assume you want to change in the car, so none of your big, bad biker friends see you in your citizen suit."

Christ, she makes me laugh.

This woman is *everything*. She knows me. Understands me in a way no one else does.

"Not yet," I say, echoing her words from a few minutes ago. My hand lands on her leg again, pushing her skirt up. And once again, she stops me.

"Stop. It's a surprise."

"What is?"

She huffs an annoyed breath and slowly slides the bottom of her dress up until bare thigh comes into view.

"They're these special, suspender, crotchless tight-thingies. To give *you* access without ripping them on me."

Those are the hottest words that have ever come out of my woman's mouth.

I run my hand over the back of my neck a few times before speaking. "Fuck me, you been running around with a bare pussy all night?"

She snorts. "No. An itty-bitty thong for-"

"Get in the back."

Her jaw drops. "What?"

I open my door and step out, hurrying to open the back door and slide into the backseat. "Get back here."

She giggles the whole time she's unbuckling her seatbelt and climbing over the middle console.

"Don't flash your ass to the parking lot," I warn.

"Shut up," she says, laughing even harder.

After a lot of muttering, cursing, and huffing, she plants her feet on the floor and rests her butt on the edge of the console. She's hunched over so her head doesn't hit the roof. "Now what?"

I pat my hands on my thighs and raise an eyebrow. "Come tell me what you want for Christmas, little girl."

"Oh my God." She bursts out laughing, the sound echoing in the interior of the SUV. "Are you going to show me your pole, Mr. *North*?"

"I'm not only going to show it to you, I'm going to give it to you. Hard."

More laughter. I could listen to that sound all night long.

I reach down, grabbing her left foot and quickly slip her

boot off, then take the other one, setting them to the side. "Lean back."

"How? I don't have a lot of space to work with here."

Ignoring the question, I slide my hands under her dress and the tight slip she's wearing underneath, bunching them up around her waist. Finally, I'm able to feast on the sight in front of me. "Jesus, these are sexy as fuck." I reach out and trace my fingers along one wide suspender and brush my knuckles against the thin thong barely covering her pussy.

She gasps and jerks her hips.

"Fuck, you're wet. I knew you were lying before."

Dipping my head, I flick my tongue over her plump lips, inhaling her scent.

She slides her fingers through my hair, lightly scratching my scalp and lets out a little moan.

"You bought these for me?"

"Yes," she answers in a breathy whisper.

I slip a finger between the thong and her skin, pulling the material to the side. I'm intoxicated by her and I take a few long, slow licks.

Call it selfish, but I want to look in her eyes when I make her come and as spontaneous and romantic as it might be to go at it in the backseat like teenagers, my current position is uncomfortable as fuck.

She whimpers when I raise my head and sit back. "Rock?"

"Right here, Baby Doll." I make quick work of my belt and shove my pants and boxers down enough to free my cock. Grinning, I grab her hand and tug her closer. "Be a good girl and get on my *pole*."

She snorts at the joke but eagerly straddles my lap. I cup her cheek and pull her closer for a kiss. Our tongues slide together hard and demanding. My free hand slides over her slick pussy, pushing the thong out of my way. I'm tempted to rip it off, but can't spare the extra couple seconds.

Her fingers wrap around my cock and I thrust into her hand a few times until she's moaning into my mouth. "Take me, Hope."

She shifts and I groan so loud as she slides down we can probably be heard inside the club.

Her moan of pleasure turns to a gasp and she freezes.

"Shh." I place my hands on her cheeks and press a rough kiss to her lips. "Easy. You set the pace. I'm all yours."

She runs her hand down my chest as she takes me deeper into her body. After a few strokes, she tugs at the tie around my neck, pulling it free and unbuttoning my shirt. In her eagerness, a few buttons go flying. One pings off the window with a soft click, but she doesn't seem to notice.

My woman—the sexiest woman in the whole damn world—ripping my clothes off because she's so crazed to get to me. Pretty much feeling like king of the world right here in the back seat of my own truck.

Her fingers trail down my chest, tracing lines of muscle. Her gentle feathery touch combined with the rough way she's grinding down on me flips my need to *desperate-to-come* in an instant.

"Hope."

I grip her hips, fingers digging in and holding her tight. Her breathing breaks into heavy panting and she clings to my shoulders. My hips pump in time with hers.

"*Ohmygod.* Right there. Please." A bunch of other words come tumbling out of her mouth. I can't keep track of anything but the incredible friction of our bodies.

We're both moving hard and fast, probably shaking the whole damn vehicle, so anyone outside can tell what we're up to. But I can't find a fuck to give.

I need her tits in my hands. Thank fuck for the forgiving, stretchy material of her sweater dress.

Up and off it goes.

"Rock," she gasps and slows down, crossing her arms over her chest.

"Baby, the windows are tinted black. No one's seeing inside." As if I'd ever allow anyone else to see what's mine.

I pry her hands off her chest and place them back on my shoulders, then tug the cups of her bra down so I can fill my hands with her breasts. "Better," I mumble, pulling her forward to slick my tongue over the tip of her nipple and tease it between my teeth.

"Oh!"

Her back arches as I claim her other breast. Hips jerking, I thrust up inside her again and she finally comes apart with a long, low cry of pleasure.

Everything inside me just explodes as I pump into her with a ragged groan.

She collapses against me, both of us sweaty and breathing hard. My arms wrap around her, holding her tight while our racing hearts calm and our breathing evens out.

After a few minutes, I reach behind us, hand flailing in the empty space for the paper towels I know I keep stored back there. “What’s wrong?” she mumbles against my neck.

“Paper towels. Back there. Clean up.” Fuck, but she’s stolen my ability to speak coherent sentences.

I groan when she eases off my spent cock and bends over the back seat, searching for the towels. Can’t help slapping her gorgeous ass that’s right in my face a few times either.

“Hey!” she yelps, finally returning to me. She drops the towels in my lap and I yank off a bunch and start cleaning us up. I probably grope her a little more than necessary in the process and she laughs.

“Didn’t have enough yet?”

“Never.”

“Where’d my dress go?”

I point to the front seat and she leans back to grab it. I watch her fix herself up, completely mesmerized. Or stupefied. I reach out, running my hand up her leg while she slips her boots back on. “These are hot, but I’m still shredding them later.”

“I expect nothing less, Rock.”

When she’s dressed, she sits next to me and hands me my jeans and long-sleeve Henley.

“Thanks, Baby Doll.”

“Purely selfish reasons. I want to see you naked.”

I chuckle, then groan as she leans down to help me kick off my shoes and work my pants down. She bites her lip as she watches me pull on the jeans and button them.

“Damn, I’m lucky,” she mutters.

“So am I.”

Once I'm finally dressed, I reach over and gently rest my hand on her hip, pulling her close. My other hand brushes her hair out of her eyes. I take in her red cheeks and flushed chest with a measure of pride. The hand on her hip strays to her belly. "You okay? I didn't hurt you, did I?"

"No, Rock. I'm fine."

Shit, even her patient, I'm-humoring-you voice turns me the fuck on. We better get inside before I decide to skip this party altogether.

As if she can hear my thoughts, she cocks her head toward the club. "Hurry up. Wrath's probably wondering where you are."

The second I step outside, she hands me my cut and I slip it on. She leaves her coat in the car and when I protest, she shakes her head. "I'm overheated. I'll be fine. It's a short walk."

I pull her Property Patch out and have her slip it on before taking her hand and walking across the parking lot. She stops me at the last second before I pull the door open.

"Wait. Is there anything I shouldn't say or do tonight?"

I give it a second of thought before answering. "No, Baby Doll."

"I don't want to stick my foot in my mouth in front of people you do business with."

I can't help grinning. "That's the beauty of this. You're the president's wife. You can't say anything wrong."

Well, obviously that's not *entirely* true. But nothing out of Hope's mouth could ever be that bad. She wouldn't be my old lady if I had to worry about her starting trouble with a few poorly chosen words.

My answer seems to satisfy her—for a second. Then she says something that makes me laugh again. "Now, Rock. We both know I'm expected to sit quiet and look pretty." Her mouth twists with a sort of wry indignation I love about Hope.

I'm stopped from answering by the door swinging open, almost knocking us down. Wrath pokes his head out and grins when he sees us. "About time."

He takes a step back so we can enter. Arms crossed over his chest and smug smile in place, he greets us, "Evening, kids."

Behind him Trinity laughs and pokes him in the side. "Don't."

"Don't what?" Hope asks with an edge to her voice. I'm pretty sure she knows what's coming.

"Saw you pull in like an hour ago." He jerks his head toward the parking lot. "The truck was rockin' so I didn't dare come knockin'."

Hope bursts out laughing and shakes her head. "I don't know what you're talking about."

"He's lying. He wanted to peek. I made him come inside," Trinity informs us.

Wrath glances down, and pulls her to his side. "Don't tell stories, angel."

"Knock it off," I growl.

As usual, none of my warnings or threats has an effect on Wrath. His lips twitch into a smirk. "You need a stronger suspension kit on your big cage. A vehicle that size shouldn't shake and wobble so much."

"God, you're an asshole."

Hope's cheeks are red, but she's laughing. "You know, Wrath." She crosses her arms over her chest and cocks her head, mirroring his earlier pose. "It's kind of creepy the way you keep spying on us."

"*Spying*. You wish. You can't spy on people who jump on each other as much as you two do."

"We took the bike," Trinity says, interrupting Hope and Wrath's banter. She holds up a backpack. "Come with me to the dressing room, Hope?"

"Sure." She tries to follow Trinity, but I don't let her go of her.

Instead, I pull her to me for a quick kiss. "Don't let any of the girls give you shit." I nod to a spot across from the dressing room. "One of us will be waiting outside to escort you into the party."

The no-bullshit tone I use makes it clear I'm not fucking around and she nods. "Got it, Mr. President."

Wrath slaps my shoulder after the girls leave. "Have fun playing dutiful, citizen husband tonight?"

"Fuck off." I point down the hallway that leads into the main area of the club "You do anything useful since you got here? Or were you waiting around all night to bust my balls?"

"Both." He gives me a smug smile. "I'm a multi-tasker."

"You're a dick."

"Christ you're cranky for a guy who just—"

"Don't finish that thought."

"You holding church back here, fuckers?" Z shouts as he walks down the hall toward us.

"How's it lookin'?" I ask.

"Like I been here all fuckin' day and I want to go home," Z says.

"Oh, what a hardship, watching the pretty, naked girls twirl around the poles all day long." Wrath's whiny imitation of Z wouldn't be complete without the fake tear he wipes away to really drive home his point.

Z's unfazed and shoves his middle finger in Wrath's face.

"I don't know why everyone's worried about us having kids," I grumble. "I have two overgrown children right in front of me."

That straightens Z out. "Malik's on the door. Dex is on his way. Teller won't be here until later, but I'm not holding my breath."

"Great, that's all we need—Whisper asking why she's not here," Wrath grumbles.

"Fuck him," Z says. "What's Teller supposed to do, drag her down here by her hair?"

"What are your plans tonight?" Wrath asks.

Z shrugs. "Get my dick sucked and go home."

"For fuck's sake," Wrath groans. "I didn't need to hear that. Now I feel all sorry for you and shit."

"Don't be jealous."

"That I have a home and the woman I want to go home with? Trust me, brother. I don't envy your situation *at all.*"

Something about Wrath's words make me glance at the dressing room door again. *Fuck me, why didn't this occur to me sooner?* "Please tell me Lexi isn't working this party."

Z eyeballs the ceiling, the walls, basically anywhere but my face before answering. "Prez, she's been good. I haven't had any issues with her since the tape thing. She knows how to handle herself with these guys. What was I supposed to do?"

"Giving me a heads up woulda been nice."

"Sorry."

"Apologize to Hope, not me."

Wrath's phone goes off and he leaves to take the call somewhere quieter.

"I'm sorry I forgot about the—"

"Forget it."

"You still plannin' to introduce Stump to Loco?"

We'd already discussed this at church last week. Stump's crew is interested in returning to moving heavier stuff that we still didn't want to touch. I wanted Loco to have first crack at the action. If the introductions went well, I was hoping it would free up some of our supply so we could sell to Stump.

But with gangsters and outlaws at the table, you never know which way negotiations might go.

You think I'd be embarrassed about whatever Wrath claims to have seen in the parking lot. By now I've come to expect his antics, so I don't give his teasing a lot of consideration after Trinity drags me away.

"What do you plan to do for your man later?" Trinity cracks up and it takes her a few seconds to spit out the rest of her words. "Since you've already ridden the *North Pole* tonight."

"Ha. Ha. You're hysterical." I shove her into the dressing room, closing the door behind us. "You and your husband should take your comedy show on the road."

Not that I make a habit out of visiting Crystal Ball, but I don't think I've ever been in the dressing room before. It's cleaner than I expected. Still looks like a cross between a sorority bathroom and a porn set. Or what I imagine those two things would look like merged together.

There are ten stations. Five on each side. A counter runs the length of the room, with drawers underneath and a long mirror above it. Only three of the stations have names on them. "Swan" is to our left. My stomach rolls when I read the next name. "Lexi."

I haven't run into her since before our wedding, when *someone* anonymously sent me an ancient sex tape featuring Lexi and Rock. *Yuck.* Part of me hoped the girl didn't work here anymore. Surely there's a shelf life for strippers?

Trinity touches my arm. She was there the day I received the video. She doesn't need to say a word. Her gentle strength is enough.

My gaze swings to the other side of the room. Only one station with a name on that side. "Regan."

The rest of the areas have stuff scattered all over them, but no names to claim them.

In the back—for the shy girls, I suppose—are a few curtained off areas and a private bathroom. From behind the sparkly pink curtains comes a few loud, giggly voices.

"Are we allowed to—*you know*—in the back rooms

tonight?" a girl asks.

"It's a private party. Anything goes," another girl we can't see answers. "If you have any issues, flag a bouncer."

"I want to get that big, blond, scary one alone in VIP," a third girl says.

Next to me, Trinity goes rigid. I glance over and she rolls her eyes.

"I highly doubt Wrath'll be interested in either of you. Besides, he's married," a female voice warns. There's no hint of an accent, so it can't be Swan back there defending Wrath.

"So?" the first girl says.

Someone snorts. "His wife's here. Give it a try. She'll probably kick the stuffing out of you."

Trinity nods and crosses her arms over her chest.

"Who is that?" I mouth at her and she shrugs in response.

The suspense is killing me, so I noisily spill the contents of my purse onto one of the counters. "My hair looks like it's been in a tornado."

"No surprise," Trinity says, coming up behind me and setting her stuff on the chair in front of us.

"Just do your job. If you cause trouble, Z will blacklist you from any future parties," Wrath's defender warns as she backs out of the curtained room.

"Whatever. The *un*married ones better be as hot."

The girl snorts in disgust. Realizing she's not alone in the room, she glances up and freezes.

Her light brown hair is longer and her left arm has a full

sleeve of tattoos now, but otherwise she's as tiny, perky, and pretty as I remember. *Lexi.*

Trinity and Lexi stare at each other in surprise. After a few seconds, Trinity blows out a breath. "Hi, Lexi." She nods toward the curtain. "Thanks."

Lexi blinks. Her gaze swings to me, then back to Trinity. Some of her nervousness seems to evaporate and she smooths her hands over her short red, plaid skirt. "Yeah, well, Wrath may be a cranky jerk, but whenever he pulls a shift here, he looks after us. Doesn't let the customers get away with any bullshit." She hurries to add, "None of the guys do. But I don't like them sayin' shit like that about..." She drifts off and her gaze lands on me again. "Hi, Hope."

Desperate for a way to make this whole situation less awkward, I nod toward the vanity where I dumped all of my stuff. "Is it okay to use this one? It doesn't have a name."

"Oh. Sure. That's fine. If you want to leave anything back here, let me know. You can use my locker."

"Thanks."

Trinity throws me a desperate look and I remember she came in here to change.

Swan and a girl I don't recognize burst into the room saving us from any more awkward moments with Lexi.

I think Lexi's almost as relieved as I am.

"You're here!" Swan shouts, giving me a big hug. She hugs Trinity too and then introduces us to the girl I don't recognize, Regan.

The two who'd been hiding behind the curtain in the back join us. I assume the red-faced one is the one who wanted to bang Wrath, because she won't look Trinity in the eye.

Lexi introduces us as "Wrath's wife and The Owner's wife." I guess she doesn't want to share our first names and I'm kinda okay with that.

The girls are dressed in little more than velvet bikinis and I sort of laugh to myself that earlier tonight I was concerned my own dress might be too revealing.

After they leave, Trinity briefly touches my arm. "I'm going to change." She raises an eyebrow, silently asking if I'm all right with being left alone for a few minutes.

"I'm good. Go on, I can't wait to see this dress."

Regan sits at her vanity to make herself up for her shift. Swan goes over the schedule for the night. I plop down into one of the chairs to fix my hair and makeup while I wait for Trinity.

A few minutes later, Trinity calls me over to the dressing room. "What do you think?" she asks, running her hands over the deep purple velvet dress hugging her curves.

"I think I'm really jealous of your ass."

She snorts. "I'm serious. Too much? Not enough?" She glances down. "It hits beneath the knees. Too conservative for a strip club?"

I stifle a laugh and look her over more carefully. "The deep V-neck and tight fit balance the length."

"It's nice and stretchy," she says, plucking at the material at her hip.

"It molds to your sensational butt very nicely. Has Wrath seen it yet?"

Instead of answering, she hugs me. "You always say the

most ridiculous stuff. I love you."

"What'd I say? Oh, your butt? I can't help it."

"I keep telling you to do more squats."

"They hurt."

"No pain no gain, Hope."

"I'd punch you right now if I didn't love you so much," I grumble.

She slips her "Property of Wrath" vest on and a pair of sparkling gold heels. "Good?"

Swan joins us, pushing the curtain wider. "Love the dress. Let me style your hair?" she asks, grabbing Trinity's hand and not waiting for an answer. "I brought the ginger ale and cranberry juice for you two. Dex stocked everything behind the bar," she says in a rush.

"Thanks for doing this. I know you're busy tonight," Trinity says.

Swan plays with a few sections of Trinity's windblown waves. "It will help calm me down."

Swan's been dancing here for a few years now. She also teaches the yoga class Trinity and I take twice a week. So her jittery demeanor tonight baffles me. "Are you nervous?"

"A little. Z asked me to perform the routine I did at nationals. I told him it had to be in costume and there would be no stripping."

Trinity snickers. "How'd he take that?"

Part of me wonders if at some point tonight, Z will ask me to stop giving his employees negotiating tips.

"He said 'the fuckers can handle six minutes of no skin.'"

From what I've seen of Swan's costume, there's not much material. And since it's mostly flesh-toned, if the guys are drunk enough, I doubt they'll be able to tell the difference. It probably wasn't a difficult decision for Z.

"Z's been telling everyone about our girl who made it to the National Pole Dancing championships," Regan adds without turning around, but in the mirror, I see her grinning.

Lexi lets out a whoop and jumps up and down. "I wish I could've gone to see you."

The more I've gotten to know Swan, I've found her to be nothing but sweet and I'm happy the girls seem to support her here. I'm a little ashamed to admit I expected more cat fighting than camaraderie.

Swan works fast, taking a large-barrel curler to Trinity's hair, then pulling it into a pretty, braided-curly design.

As she's sliding in the final bobby pin, the volume of the music in the club increases.

"I can finish if you need to get ready, Swan," Trinity offers.

"I do need to change."

"You don't mind us watching, right?" I ask. I'm not sure why.

Swan tilts her head and blinks a few times before answering. "Of course not, Hope."

"Rock's going to break the door down if we don't get out there soon," Trinity says, nudging me toward the door.

"Hey," Z greets us when we emerge. He's leaning against the wall across from the dressing room door. "Rock needed to take care of something," he explains.

"Thank you, Z. I'm sure you have more important things to do than wait for us," I say, taking the arm he offers.

"Walk around the club with two pretty girls on my arms?" He shakes his head. "Nope. Nothing more important than that."

"Swan said she's doing her routine tonight."

"She drives a hard bargain," he says with a wry twist of his lips but no hint of irritation in his tone.

He leads us to a large, round booth in the back corner of the club. The exact spot I'd expect Rock to pick so he can survey everything going on in the club from a distance.

One of Sway's guys I recognize from Downstate, says hello before disappearing with a dancer into one of the back rooms.

I spot Serena sort of idly wandering the floor by herself and drag Trinity over to say hello.

Serena's eyes widen when we approach. "Hi. I was hoping you'd be here tonight," she says with a nervous half-smile.

"We're here."

"Shadow dragged me with him, but then he disappeared with one of the dancers as soon as we walked in the door." She rolls her eyes. "I really don't want to be stranded."

"Rock and I took his truck. We can give you a ride if you need it."

Trinity turns and her narrow-eyed-raised-eyebrow expression clearly says, 'Are you insane?' but I'm not sure why.

"Oh." Serena bites her lip and drops her gaze to the floor. "Thank you so much, Hope. I'll be fine. But thank you."

Willow ends up pulling Serena behind the bar with her, and Trinity shakes her head.

"What'd I do wrong?"

"Where *exactly* are you and Rock giving her a ride *to*?"

"I don't know."

"Having her up at the clubhouse is probably going to upset Heidi," Trinity says gently.

My hand flies up, covering the, "oh shit," that spills out of my mouth. Immediate guilt washes over me. I never considered that. How could I be so stupid?

"Dammit," I grumble. "How am I supposed to remember every wick the guys have dipped their dicks in?"

Trinity snort-laughs loud enough that people turn and stare at us.

I'm still glaring at her when she stops laughing and her expression turns serious. She places her hand on my arm. "You've always treated all the girls fairly." She taps a finger against my vest. "It's what makes you a good first lady."

"Heidi's *family*," I protest. She's the spunky little sister I never had but always wanted.

"I meant—" she waves her hands in the air "—the rest of them."

"Oh."

She glances around the room. "I'm not supposed to tell you this, but Rock's taking you away for the weekend. You're not going home tonight. So, if any of the girls need a ride somewhere, send them to me and I'll arrange it."

I'm not surprised by her admission. In fact, after a night of heavy socializing, I figured Rock would want to cuddle up in the house together or spend time doing something outdoorsy. I'm not even curious about where he's taking me, because as long as I'm with him, it doesn't matter. "Thank you."

Her attention strays to something behind me and she nods her head. "Rock's looking for you. I'm going to help Willow out. If you see Wrath, let him know where I am."

Even though Rock's all the way across the room, electricity zips down my spine when I turn and meet his simmering gaze. I want to run over to him, but I take my time moving through the room until I'm by his side.

He pulls me closer with an arm around my waist. "Hope, I want to introduce you to Malik. He's considering life as a prospect."

"Oh." I'd been so focused on my husband I didn't notice the mountain of a man he's standing next to, which I guess says something either about how daft I am or how stunning my husband is. I'm not sure.

I look up. Way, way up. Malik's easily Wrath's size, but in every other way they're opposite. Well, except for the air of menace that surrounds him.

While Malik's expression is bland, his keen, dark-cinnamon eyes seem to have a thousand opinions. "Considering?" I hold out my hand. "I guess that's why you still get to have a first name instead of being called "hey, prospect."

Black eyebrows shoot up and his full lips curve into a hint of a smile. He takes my hand, giving it a surprisingly gentle shake for his size. "Nice to meet you, First Lady. You need anything tonight and your man's busy, let me know."

"Thank you."

Rock and Malik sort of nod at each other. They seem to

share a mutual respect. Whether they actually *like* each other, I can't determine.

Rock leads me back inside, but stops in a quiet corner near the end of the bar. "Everything, okay?"

"I'm fine."

Trinity taps my shoulder and hands me a virgin poinsettia to drink.

Willow wags a finger between us. "Are one of you pregnant?"

I snort into my drink and answer without looking up. "Rock doesn't like me tipsy before he has his way with me."

Trinity howls with laughter.

Behind me, Rock's body rumbles and his hand slides down to cup my ass. "Absolutely true."

"There you are," Wrath says, sweeping Trinity into his arms. She reaches up and whispers something in his ear. "Hey, Rock?" Wrath shouts. "You need me right now?"

"No."

He drags Trinity away from the bar. "We'll be right back."

Willow sighs and leans her elbows on the bar. "They're so cute together."

The front door opens and a blast of cold air wafts in. Rowdy male voices reach us a split second before the men come into view. "Sway's here, goodie," I mumble into my glass.

Rock's hold on me tightens, but he welcomes Sway's group warmly—well as warm as Rock gets.

Sway's gaze sweeps over me. "What? You, couldn't let your man out alone one night to have some fun?"

Neither of us dignify that with an answer.

I'm introduced to Steer, who I've met before. The rest of the guys I recognize, but immediately forget their names. They take seats closer to the stage so I doubt I'll be speaking to them again tonight.

More girls swarm around us. A few pretend not to notice me. Rock gives them a cold glare and they back off. Sway's more than happy to accept the extra attention.

"Where'd Trin go?" Z asks, brushing against my other side.

"Wrath dragged her away."

He surveys the room and shrugs. "They better not be in my office."

"Why would they—never mind." I attempt to cover my laughter with a hand over my mouth, but fail miserably.

Z shakes his head before stalking away.

"What crawled up his ass?" Sway asks.

CHAPTER TEN

Trinity

IT TAKES A LOT OF CONCENTRATION TO CARRY ON A conversation when your husband has the remote control to your underwear.

The thought makes me snicker.

"What's up with you?" Willow asks. "You've been grinning like a fool all night."

I shrug and shake my head. Willow and I haven't reached the sharing-stories-about-our-sex-toys stage of our friendship yet. I don't even think I'd tell Hope about this one and I tell her almost everything.

Once again, Wyatt's proved what a clever devil he is. Except for when I was in the dressing room with Hope—when Wyatt swore he wouldn't mess with the remote—I haven't had a second to think about anything other than what his next move will be.

Every knowing look he sends my way makes my panties wet.

Despite the Spanx under my dress, at some point the gadget shifts. The next time Wrath flicks it on, I barely feel a thing.

I suppose I could keep quiet. But that sort of feels like cheating at our private game.

My gaze travels around the club not finding my husband anywhere.

"I think he's outside with Ravage," Serena says, hopping onto one of the bar stools.

Turning around, I force a smile on my lips.

She raises an eyebrow. "Wrath. I don't think he's getting a lap dance or anything. I've never even seen him look at another girl."

Willow hip-checks me. "You two are inspiration for girls everywhere."

"What?"

"Hot, overprotective, worships the ground you walk on, *and* faithful," Willow says. She glances over at Hope and Rock. "Now, Rock's all those things, *plus* outright obsessed with his wife." She laughs and slaps four shot glasses on the bar. "Tequila?" she asks.

"Uh, no." There's no way I'm drinking when Wrath and I are engaged in a game of orgasm chicken.

Before Willow tries to talk me into a drink, I pour two ginger ale and cranberry juice and hand one off to Hope.

Wrath finally shows up, crooked grin in place. I swear I almost combust at the sight of him.

Especially when he leans down to whisper in my ear, "I forgot to tell you how pretty you look tonight."

The warmth and sweetness in his voice seems at odds with his Viking-biker appearance. Maybe that's why it's extra swoony. "Thank you."

He runs his hands over my hips and ass. "You need more things in this material."

Chuckling, I turn, catching him for a quick kiss. "There's a problem in paradise."

He raises an eyebrow.

"There's a malfunction. *Down there.*"

He still seems confused, but checks to see if Rock needs him and then pulls me away.

"Where are we going?" I ask.

"Somewhere private."

At first I'm worried he means the VIP rooms, but he steers us in the opposite direction, heading for Z's office. He pulls out a key and flicks on the light before pushing me inside.

"What's going on?"

I point to my crotch. "Your little torture device isn't working right."

He barks out a laugh. "Torture device. Tell me you're not loving it."

I glance away, because we both know I'd be lying.

"You didn't want to adjust it yourself?" he asks.

Placing my hands on my hips, I narrow my eyes. "I didn't

think you'd like your wife shoving her hand down her panties in front of everyone."

"Good call."

"Everything okay out there?" I ask.

"Yeah. Waiting to see who else shows up."

"Ugh. Tawny's not coming, is she?"

He gives me an *are you serious* look. "Fuck no. Sway wouldn't bring her to this when there's so much free pussy running around."

I give him a little kick for the "free pussy" comment. "*You're* not hoping for a lap dance later?" I tease.

He takes the question more seriously then I intended. "Only woman I want dancing on my dick is *you* and you can do that at home."

"You don't want a private dance from your wife in the gladiator room?"

He cocks an eyebrow. "There isn't enough disinfectant in this club to make me take you in there. You wanna pole dance for me, I'm more than happy to install one in our bedroom, Angel Face."

I throw my head back and laugh. "You better not let Z overhear you say that. You'll hurt his feelings."

"Quit stalling and hike up that dress so I can take care of my pussy."

"Your pussy," I grumble, wiggling the dress up around my hips and wriggling my Spanx off.

He cups my face with his hand and places a rough kiss on my lips. "Try and deny it."

"Nope," I whisper.

"Good, now get up on the desk so I can fix it so we can

go back to the party." He cocks his head and a there's a devious curve to his lips. "If you're a good girl, I'll even let you come."

I drape myself over the desk and put my feet up the way he asks.

"One of the snaps came loose," he mumbles and curses as he fixes it, the whole time ratcheting my excitement higher and higher.

A few seconds later, he flicks it on and I jump. "Shit! It's working now."

It goes up another notch.

"Oh, fuck."

"That's right," he encourages in a low voice. He presses a kiss to my knee and strokes my inner thighs with his hands.

I lose track of time, lose track of everything except the steady, glorious buzz, Wyatt's firm touch and commanding voice.

"Wyatt." I reach for him and he takes my hand.

"Come on. Let go for me, Trinity," he whispers.

My head falls back and I'm not sure what he's up to until he lifts my hips and slams into me. He thrusts hard and deep. There's no time to brace myself or appreciate the fullness of him.

"Oh my God!"

"No, just me, Angel Face."

I can't help laughing and I reach up to touch his face. He leans into my palm and closes his eyes for a second. I curl my other hand around his forearm.

"That's right. Hold onto me," he urges. "Let yourself go. Come for your husband."

He fucks faster, hammering into me with long, deep strokes.

So much pressure builds, racing through me and finally bursting into intense pleasure. I let out a low, guttural groan as wave after wave washes over me. My body jerks as I glance up and find Wyatt's eyes pinned on me. So many emotions without having to say a word.

He keeps thrusting until he comes with a long groan of satisfaction.

WRATH

I NEED a second to figure out where I am. I've been painfully hard most of the night thinking about the little vibrator snuggled up next to Trinity's clit. It was only a matter of time before I dragged her into a private room to fuck her senseless.

That she so sweetly told me about the malfunction and wanted me to fix it was the real kicker. I never needed to fuck her more than I did that second.

"Oh, for fuck's sake!" Z shouts behind me. "What the fuck, Wrath?"

"Get out!"

I couldn't give a fuck less if he sees my bare ass, but I don't want him embarrassing Trinity.

The door slams shut and Trinity falls back on the desk,

covering her face with her hands. At first I think she's crying, but the hysterical noises coming out of her are laughter.

"Oh my God. Poor Z." She laughs even harder.

When she finally catches her breath, she hops off the desk and leans up to kiss me. "Thank you for letting me come," she purrs.

Z might be out of luck and waiting out there for a while.

I help her clean up and put herself back together before fixing myself up. She smooths her hair back into place and raises an eyebrow.

"All straightened out." I circle my finger over her chest and cheeks. "Except for the freshly fucked glow you've got going on."

"That, I'll wear proudly."

"Hey." I curl my arm around her waist, clapping my hand over her ass, and haul her against me. "Thank you."

"For?"

"Letting me be a filthy beast with you."

She lets out a soft sigh and reaches up to kiss me again. "I love my filthy beast-man."

I hug her tighter and make a few growly noises against her throat until she's laughing and pushing me away.

"Seriously!?" Z shouts from the other side of the door.

Trinity chokes on her laughter and waves her hand at the door. Keeping my arm around her, I open it and face a pissed-off Z.

"My desk? Really? Weren't you just bragging about having a house to fornicate in?"

Like the dick I love being, I scratch my chin. "I'd say

sorry, but I'd be lying."

"Get out of here." He pushes past us and slams the door behind him.

Trinity's gaze darts to the door. "You think he's really that mad at us?"

"No. He's mad at *me*. And he'll get over it."

I test the remote and she jumps. "Jesus, Wyatt, give a girl a second to recover."

"Just making sure it's working, Trin." I lean down and brush my lips against her ear. "And reminding you whose pussy that is."

CHAPTER ELEVEN

Hope

"Come on, Sway," Rock says. "I have a table set up in the back."

Wrath and Trinity meet us on the way over, both of them flushed and sweaty-looking.

I nudge Trin with my elbow. "What were you two up to?"

She jumps even though we're standing right next to each other. "Nothing. Why?"

"No reason." I reach around and extract something shiny out of her hair—which is much fuzzier looking than it was twenty minutes ago. "Were you two rolling around on Z's desk?" I ask in my sternest mom voice, holding the paper clip in front of her face.

"Don't judge me, *backseat* baby doll."

My jaw drops. "What did you call me?"

She tilts her head and stares at me until we both start laughing. Wrath glances down at us and raises an eyebrow. His questioning expression turns to devious when Trinity plucks the paper clip out of my hand and thrusts it in his face.

He takes it and shoves it his pocket.

Trinity jolts again and I give her the side-eye. "Are you practicing your dance moves, twitchy?"

"What? No."

Rock nudges me into the booth first and Trinity ends up on my other side. I have the impression Wrath and Rock planned out our seating arrangements ahead of time to keep anyone else away from us.

Sway doesn't stay with us long. The girl who'd been in the dressing room earlier hoping to hook up with Wrath ends up grinding on Sway's lap for a few songs before leading him into one of the back rooms with a bottle of champagne.

Z ends up taking Sway's seat.

"Do you have to use a blacklight to clean up the VIP rooms?" I ask Z, who smirks at the question.

"And a lot of bleach," he adds.

Rock's questioning eyes meet mine. "You mad?"

"About Sway cheating on his wife? Couldn't care less." I consider some of the conversations I've had with Tawny in the past. "I'm sure she's having her own jolly time with some unsuspecting elf right about now anyway. That's their business."

Z spits out the beer he'd just taken a sip of and Rock chokes.

Trinity has her head buried against Wrath's shoulder, shaking with laugher and Wrath just clucks his tongue at me. "Cinderella. What have we done to you?"

I raise an eyebrow, hoping he'll explain.

"I have a feeling before us, you would've been outraged on Tawny's behalf," he says.

"There are probably lots of things I never did before I met Rock." I lean over and whisper in Rock's ear. "For example, I never wore crotchless tights before I met you."

He groans and closes his eyes.

The Wolf Knights MC joins us next and Wrath's the one to greet them, and bring them to our table.

After they leave, Rock leans in closer. "You know I can't stop thinking about what's under your dress," he murmurs against my ear.

"That's why it was supposed to be a *surprise* for later."

His hand lands on my leg, keeping a firm, possessive grip while someone else comes over to demonstrate their obsequience to the King.

Z taps Rock's arm and juts his chin toward the door. "Look sharp, Prez."

Reaching down, Rock takes my hand and pulls me out of the booth with him.

The tall, wiry black man he stops in front of definitely isn't a biker. At least I can't picture anyone in a bright red suit, white shirt and black tie on a motorcycle. On anyone else, it would probably be a garish imitation of a Santa suit, but this guy makes it work. The two beautiful women on either side of him don't hurt either. His wild eyes land on Rock and he breaks into a big smile, holding his arms out and shooing his companions away.

I'm close enough to both feel and hear the growl in Rock's throat. He's normally a quick handshake sort of guy with non-Lost Kings. But he tolerates the brotherly hug and backslap from this man for about three whole seconds before pulling back.

"Mr. North! You finally trust me enough to invite me to one of your VIP events."

Rock heaves out a sigh. "You've been here plenty of times, Loco." He gestures to me. "This is my wife, Hope."

I extend my hand and he grabs it, bringing it to his lips in an unexpected gentlemanly way.

"The pleasure is all mine, Mrs. North."

"Ah, thank you, mister…?"

"Loco. Everyone calls me Loco."

"Okay." I glance at Rock for confirmation and he nods. His head's probably about to explode since Loco's lips are still hovering over the back of my hand. "It's nice to meet you, Loco. Thank you for joining us."

Finally, he drops my hand and straightens up, focusing his attention on Rock.

"I ran into Black Wrath outside. Where's Original Wrath?"

I have to duck my head to hide my snort of laughter. This man's either ballsy or crazy.

Rock shows him to our table, and Wrath's surprisingly friendly. Well, friendly for Wrath.

"Mrs. Wrath! Nice to see you."

"Hi, Loco," Trinity says, waving at him, but not moving from Wrath's side.

Rock and Loco speak in low tones, but I catch Sparky's name a few times.

"Is Sparky here yet?" I ask.

Rock glances up and nods. "He's in the break room."

"Oh, good." I worry about Sparky spending so much time in the basement.

Wrath leans over to join Rock and Loco's conversation, sort of squishing Trinity against me. "Let's go dance," she says, grabbing my hand. Wrath stands to let us out of the booth.

I have no intention of doing anything resembling dancing in a building full of half-naked, younger, professional dancers, but it's a relief to get away from the men so they can "discuss business."

ROCK

"Now that's a classy dame, Rock. Good for you," Loco says, slapping me on the back. "I feel like we've entered a new phase in our relationship here. You lettin' me near your precious and all."

"You trying to do business or date me, Loco?"

"Tonight? Neither."

"Well, reconsider, because I have someone coming I think you should meet."

He raises an eyebrow, but before he has a chance to question it, Sway joins us, patting Loco's shoulder to grab his attention.

While they talk, my gaze scans the crowd looking for Hope. She's at the bar with Trinity and Willow—exactly where I want her if she's not with me.

The DJ announces Swan's performance and Hope rushes over with Trinity in tow. Our table's more crowded now, so she ends up in my lap, which suits me fine.

"Have fun?"

"Sure. I always like talking to Willow."

"You keep the club's girls in line, Mrs. North?" Loco asks her.

Her forehead wrinkles and she shakes her head.

"You dance?"

"God, no. I'd trip over my own feet."

Loco chuckles and sits back, spreading his arms over the back of the bench and not taking his eyes off my woman, which is starting to get *real fucking annoying.*

Hope's saved from more questions and Loco's saved from me breaking his face, by the lights going down and Swan taking the stage.

CHAPTER TWELVE

MURPHY

ALEXA'S DELIGHTED TO FIND THE TREE IN FRONT OF THE living room window. I guess from her perspective a tree inside the house is pretty damn exciting all by itself. Just wait until we get it decorated.

With her head tipped back, mouth open, and wide eyes, she watches while Heidi and I unwind strings of lights and work them into the branches. Around and around.

"Should we wait and do the ornaments with Rock and Hope?" Heidi asks when we run out of lights.

"Sure. Let's see how these look though."

I plug it in, unprepared for the shrieks of joy behind me. Alexa freaking out.

"Twee! Twee!" She crawls closer and Heidi pulls her back.

"No touching. Just looking," Heidi reminds her.

"Look!"

"Yes. *Look*. No touch."

Heidi settles on the floor in front of the tree with Alexa in her lap. I stand behind Heidi and she tips her head back, resting it against my leg.

"I think she likes it," I say.

"Me too."

Eventually, I drop down next to them. "What'd you think about Charlotte offering to have us stay there for Christmas Eve?"

She nibbles on her bottom lip. "I really like the idea. Would you be okay with that?"

"I think it would be nice to let Rock and Hope have the house to themselves for Christmas Eve and Marcel would love having you guys there." I hesitate because I'm not trying to lay a guilt trip on her.

"And?"

"He missed you and Alexa last year."

She nods slowly. "Let's do it. We'll come back here and do presents in the afternoon with Rock and Hope. Then Trinity's planning a big dinner at the clubhouse for everyone. I promised I'd help her and Swan."

"Sounds like a plan."

"Wow, I feel like such a grown up."

I chuckle and pull her closer. "You've been one for a while now."

She glances down at Alexa's sleepy face and smiles.

"Yeah."

A few minutes later, Alexa conks out completely, hands fisted in Heidi's shirt and a happy smile in place.

"My legs are asleep," Heidi whispers.

"Here, I'll take her."

Gently, I lift Alexa, praying like hell I don't wake her. Together, Heidi and I put her to bed.

We return to the living room and she flops on the couch.

"Tired?" I ask.

"It was a good day."

I sit next to her and pull her against my side. "Day's not over yet."

"Are you sure you're not mad you couldn't go to the party?" Heidi asks.

The thought of spending another night of my life inside a strip club actually makes me want to vomit.

Totally normal for a guy my age, right?

But I'm perfectly content right where I am. My girl snuggled up on the couch next to me and Alexa sleeping in her room.

"Blake?" Heidi prompts when I take too long to answer.

Love Heidi so damn much, but some nights she frustrates me.

Placing two fingers on her cheek, I turn her to face me. "If I really wanted to go, I would've gone."

Her eyes widen at the simple truth.

"Spending the evening at Crystal Ball or spending all day and night with my girls? No contest. None. This is *exactly* where I want to be tonight and every night."

A hesitant smile flickers over her lips and she exhales slowly.

"What's wrong?"

"Nothing." She stops and picks at a loose thread on her jeans. "I feel restless. Like I'm supposed to be doing *something*."

"You are. Relaxing. We had a busy day." I rest my hand over hers. "You've had a pretty crazy year."

She opens her mouth, but I place one finger over her lips. "I'm really proud of you. You're balancing being a mom, going to school, your job, and you're killin' it."

"I don't feel like I'm *killin' it*," she mumbles behind my finger. "I feel like I should do more. I wouldn't be able to do any of it, if it wasn't for you." She waves her hand in the air. "Hope and Rock, my brother."

"You can do anything you put your mind to, but tonight you're going to chill with your fiancé. Alexa's sound asleep. Rock and Hope are out for the night. Trinity's studio is closed until after New Year's."

Heidi's mouth quirks at that. Turns out Trinity's as demanding to work for as Wrath. And just like Wrath never cut me any slack working for him at the gym, Trinity expects a lot from her photography assistant. Eager to prove herself, Heidi's excelled at the job—Trinity's words, not mine. Also like her husband, Trinity doesn't hand out compliments unless someone's earned them.

Her gaze wanders to the tree. Heidi wanted to wait and do the rest of the decorating with Rock and Hope.

"Since we have the place to ourselves tonight, want to

check out the hot tub?" I ask, pushing her hair off her neck and replacing it with my mouth.

"Hmm," she sighs, then giggles. "I was putting my summer clothes away yesterday, so I even know where my suit is."

I hadn't planned on wearing *anything,* but since I'm excited to get her alone in the hot tub, I keep my mouth shut. Her suit can always be removed later.

CHAPTER THIRTEEN

Hope

Until you see it for yourself, it's easy to dismiss pole dancing and say it's not a real sport. Within five seconds, it's obvious how much discipline, athleticism, strength, and grace it takes to perform. Somehow Swan makes it appear effortless.

"She's amazing," I say.

Trinity nods. "We need to step up our yoga game." She ended up in Wrath's lap, but she's close enough that we can talk without too many people overhearing us.

"Are you kidding? I'd land on my head if I attempted any of that."

Wrath's wrapped around Trinity like an anaconda with

his head buried against her shoulder—doing God only knows what that makes Trinity's eyes roll back in her head.

She's gone. I end up turning in Rock's lap to face the stage completely.

"Careful," Rock groans.

Oops.

I wiggle in his lap again and he grips my hips to stop me.

One of his arms bands around my chest and he gently grips my jaw, turning me to face the room, where not everyone who's hooking up has bothered to find some privacy. His lips brush against my ear. "This isn't *your* lawyer party. I don't need the privacy of an office upstairs or a closet. No one would think twice if I fucked you right here. Right now," he rasps.

His hand squeezes my hip, then slowly moves down over my leg. "There are three items between your pussy and my cock. It would be *so* easy to move them out of my way. When I say *careful,* I mean it."

"Uhh." A delightful shiver electrifies my skin and steals my words. I'm practically panting with excitement when he releases me.

He brushes my hair to the side and places a kiss at the base of my neck. "That's not the reaction I expected from you, Hope."

I turn, catching him off guard and brush my lips against his. "It's hot, because I trust you. You'd never fuck me in public. You're too much of a caveman to expose *your woman* that way."

His eyes widen. Along with surprise, I find humor and

heat in their steel gray depths. His gaze flicks over the crowded room then back to me. This time desire burns in his eyes. "Normally that's true." His low-spoken words reach every part of me. "But even cavemen sometimes have the urge to publicly claim their women."

ROCK

I HAVE no intention of fucking Hope out in the open, but it's always fun to tease her. Maybe I *am* feeling territorial after watching Loco salivate over my wife for the last hour. The fact that she's oblivious to his interest soothes the beast in me that wants to impale her on my cock in front of everyone.

The lights in the club brighten a fraction as Swan finishes her routine and exits the stage. A wave of rowdy whistles and cheering fills the room. I wouldn't have expected such a favorable reaction to a performance that was more artistic than naked. Not from this crowd. Z made a good call.

Loco leans in. "Talented lady you got there, Rock. She gonna work the room?"

I'm not sure what Swan's plans are for the night other than dancing on the stage. When the brothers sat down for church to discuss the party, I'd been given the impression the VIP rooms were a "no fly zone" for Swan during this event.

Searching the crowd, I locate Dex and signal him to bring Swan to the table.

Briefly I wonder if anyone bothered to tell Malik to search our guests for weapons tonight.

I glance over at Wrath, who's still busy molesting his wife, and reach over to tap his arm. He flicks his gaze my way before lifting his head and raising an eyebrow. It takes him less than five seconds to assess the situation and gently transition Trinity from his lap to the seat next to him. He places his elbows on the table and leans forward. To anyone else he looks casual. I know he's ready to pounce if anyone gets out of control.

Hope pushes out of my lap before I have a chance to stop her and brushes past Loco—who uses the opportunity to stare at her ass—to get to Swan. She throws her arms around her. "That was so amazing. I know I've watched you practice before but, wow!" she gushes.

Wrath nudges Trinity in their direction and she joins the girls.

"Not quite what I had in mind," Loco says. "But the view sure is pretty."

Wrath's irritated growl reaches me and I cut him a look that I hope he reads as *calm the hell down.*

Dex moves past the girls and addresses me. "Did you need me, Prez?"

"Loco wanted to compliment Swan's performance."

His gaze slides to Loco and they shake hands. "Swan," he says without turning around.

She appears at his side and Loco doesn't wait to be

introduced. He pulls the kissing-the-back-of-her-hand move he did with Hope and then yanks her into his lap.

Dex narrows his eyes and pulls out a chair, dropping into it and making it clear he's not going anywhere.

CHAPTER FOURTEEN

Charlotte

"What do you think?" I ask, stepping into the living room.

Marcel stops and stares. "Wow. I didn't get the whole effect before."

It took time, but I wrestled my hair into a fancier knot with lots of loose tendrils framing my face. I have a lot more makeup on than I usually wear, but it's a holiday party after all.

"I didn't think about my outfit carefully enough. My property patch will cover up all the racy cut-outs of my dress."

A deep rumble works out of him and he hooks an arm

around my waist, inching me closer. "The way it should be, Sunshine. All those sexy bits are for me."

He cups my cheeks, all playfulness disappearing as he searches my face. "Are you sure you're okay going to this party?" He hesitates. "We don't have to go if you're not comfortable," he adds in a lower voice.

His grave demeanor gives me pause and I stop to consider what he's actually asking. When I finally figure it out, I press my hand to my chest. I haven't thought about *that* night in months. Not since Marcel came home and told me he and my uncle had taken care of the second man who violated me.

I glance down at my boots, sort of amazed that this is the first year I didn't have a sense of dread the minute Christmas decorations and music started popping up everywhere. I'd actually been *looking* forward to our first Christmas together in our new house, surrounded by our family. It's the first Christmas without my mother and all I feel is *free*. Free to breathe and be happy for once.

"Hey," Marcel's hand brushes my chin, tipping my head up. "I'm sorry—"

"No," I say, cutting him off. "This is the first time since it happened that I've been excited about the holidays." I can't hide the amazement in my voice.

"I didn't mean to bring up bad stuff."

But he didn't. He reminded me of how far I've come and how much of my life I've gotten back *because* of him. Things I don't want to take for granted.

"I'm at peace this year and that's because of you."

Love will never be a strong enough word to describe

what I feel for him. I slip my arms around his waist and rest my cheek against his chest. The two of us stand there holding each other without speaking for a few heartbeats.

"I love holding you," he murmurs into my hair.

"And I love the way you hold me," I answer.

CHAPTER FIFTEEN

Hope

THE TENSION AROUND OUR TABLE RISES TO UNCOMFORTABLE levels. Well, for me. Rock seems completely calm.

Wrath has an air of exasperation around him.

It's Dex who looks like a rubber band stretched too tight.

I settle my hand on his shoulder and he reaches up and pats me. "How're you doing tonight, First Lady?" he asks without taking his eyes off Swan.

She's still sitting in Loco's lap while he compliments her performance.

"Good." I raise my voice to capture Loco's attention. "That was amazing, Swan. I've seen bits and pieces but never the full routine."

"Thank you," she says shyly.

"How long you been doing that, sweetheart?" Loco asks.

"Um." Swan covers up her nervous laughter with a hand over her mouth. "Pretty much since I could walk."

Rock clears his throat. "Swan, you have some things to take care of in back?"

It's more of an order than a question, and Swan's quick to seize the opportunity to scramble out of Loco's lap.

"What a slave-driver." Loco flashes a slow grin at Rock. "Can't let the lady have a few minutes off?"

"We run a tight ship," Dex says, standing and nudging Swan away.

"Dexter with her? That why he's lookin' so bent?" Loco asks.

Rock doesn't have to answer because Lexi joins us and is more than happy to warm Loco's lap. I brush past Loco to rejoin my husband and he pulls me down next to him. "You see what I put up with," he whispers in my ear.

Before I have a chance to answer, Lexi stands and pulls Loco toward the VIP rooms. "I'll be back, Rock," he says before following Lexi.

Rock cuts a glare at Wrath. "You seen Stump or Chaser yet?"

"Not yet. You know they'd both stop to see you first."

Trinity returns to Wrath's lap, but they both seem more alert and less playful than before.

More "traditional" pole dancing has taken over the center stage. A number of girls circulate through the crowd.

"Disgusted yet?" Rock asks.

Laughing, I shake my head.

There's a round of shouts by the front door and a few minutes later Teller and Charlotte join us.

"You came!" I say, rushing over to greet them. I hug Charlotte tight—as if I didn't just see her this morning. "We weren't sure if you would be here."

Teller shrugs. "How could we skip this?"

"How was the Bar Association party?" she asks me.

"Nice actually. We didn't stay too long. I do have something I want to talk to you about later, though."

She tilts her head and narrows her eyes, much the way I probably did when Mara suggested I co-chair one of the committees. I snort-laugh. "Later. Tell me, did you find a tree?"

"Yup," Teller answers. "Alexa flipped her shit when we chopped 'em down too."

"Aww. I'm sorry I missed that."

"Murphy got the tree set up at your house."

"Oh, he did? That's so sweet. I bet Alexa loved it."

I turn to lead Charlotte over to where Trinity and I are sitting and collide with a hard wall of a man.

"Whoa. Sorry, Hope," Whisper says, steadying me with a hand on my shoulder. "Was coming to say hello to Charlotte."

"Hey, Whisper," she says, reaching up to give him a quick hug. "How've you been?"

"Fine. Heard from your uncle this morning. He's spending the winter down in Florida."

"Oh, that's good." A nervous smile flickers over her lips and she backs up against Teller, who slings his arm over her shoulders.

Whisper's gaze slides to Teller. "Still haven't heard from Keeper yet."

Teller doesn't so much as twitch. "Sorry to hear that."

Unsure of why the atmosphere took such a weird turn, I link my arm through Teller's. "Rock's been waiting for you."

"Aw, fuck. What'd I do now?" he jokes.

"Hey," Rock calls out, standing to give Teller a quick embrace. "Glad you made it." He nods to Charlotte.

"So, what'd I miss?" Charlotte asks, shoving into the booth next to me.

"Swan's performance, a lot of bare skin, and no jolly half-naked elves for us to enjoy."

Even though Rock's deep in conversation with Teller and a brother from Sway's club, he reaches over and squeezes my leg. His subtle way of saying he heard my naked elf comment.

ROCK

GOD DAMN HAS this been a long night.

Loco returns from the VIP rooms in time to meet Stump and Chaser. Stump's interested in working with Loco, but he seems to feel he's doing me a favor and wants something in return.

He leans in lowering his voice. "I'd like to introduce you to my daughter-in-law's father. He's gonna pay us a visit in the spring for my granddaughter's graduation.

I've known Stump since I was a kid tagging along on a run with my old mentor, Grinder. That's how I know the man he's referring to is tied to the Russian mafia. Business I've never wanted to get involved with.

"I need more details."

"Another time. Tonight's for celebrating."

Then why the fuck even bring it up?

Now I'm just irritated.

I endure a few more hours of conversation, catching up with people I haven't seen in a while. Making arrangements for new deals. Scheduling things for next year.

Then I'm *done*. I need my wife and some quiet.

"I have to check in with Z, and then we'll get going," I say to Hope.

She nods and kisses my cheek. "I'll wait here. Unless you need me?"

"Nope. Here's fine." I lift my chin at Wrath. "You good?"

"We're going to head out soon too."

"Sounds good."

I glance around the club and decide I'd rather have Hope with me.

Z's nowhere in sight. One of the girls says she saw him down in the VIP rooms and I roll my eyes.

"Ooo, I've never seen the secret VIP section," Hope says, giggling and hurrying to keep up with me.

"Don't get too excited. It's not all that interesting."

Z's put a lot of effort into redesigning the VIP rooms since I used to run the place. Each room seems to have its own theme. Gaudy, over-the-top, but it's more than paid for itself according to the spreadsheets Teller hands out at church.

I find Z stumbling out of the "Roman Gladiator" themed room.

"Living out your gladiator fantasy?" I ask.

He smirks. "What's up?"

"We're leaving. You got this?"

"Who else is still here?"

I give him a rundown and he nods. "It's all good."

"You okay, Mama Bear?" Z asks Hope. "We didn't traumatize you too much, right?"

"I had fun. The club's really impressive."

"Thanks." He smiles, but it's more pained than anything and Hope gives him a tight squeeze.

"Take care of yourself, Z."

We stop at the bar so Hope can say goodnight to some of the girls. Sparky's sitting in the corner with a beer, watching Willow work. Hope hugs Sparky too. "Did you show off your babies tonight?"

"Sure did, First Lady. Did you want to see them?"

"No, you can show me at home. We're heading out."

He gives her a blissed-out smile that makes me suspect he was sampling the goods more than showing them off. But whatever. It's the holidays and I don't care.

The cold night air slaps us in the face as we step outside. A light dusting of snow covers the ground and Hope shivers as we cross the parking lot. "Sorry, Baby Doll. I should've come and picked you up."

"I'm fine." She gestures toward the rapidly falling snow. "I'm worried about Wrath and Trinity. They took the bike."

"Someone will give them a ride. He won't take any chances with her."

Once we're driving, it doesn't take her long to realize we're not headed home. She's fighting to keep the smile off her face.

"What?"

"Where are we going?"

"You already know, don't you?"

She bursts out laughing. "I don't know *where*. Just that you have something planned."

Now I feel bad, because it's not even anywhere fancy. It's a nice hotel and I reserved a large suite, but it's still in Empire. Not far from Crystal Ball.

"Don't get your hopes up."

She rests her soft hand against my arm. "Rock, I don't care where we go, as long as I'm with you. I do have one question for you, though. What am I supposed to wear for however long we're away?"

"Not a damn thing." I won't bother telling her there's a bag of her stuff in the back. Not yet anyway.

She lets out a contented sigh. "Why is that such a damn turn on?"

I drop my hand on her leg, running up under her dress until I reach bare skin. "Because your body recognizes I'm its king."

Hope's full of surprises tonight. She slides down in her seat, spreading her legs for me. "*Mmm*. Long live the king."

CHAPTER SIXTEEN

MURPHY

WHILE HEIDI SEARCHES FOR HER SUIT AND CHANGES, I CHECK on Alexa, then go outside to get the hot tub ready.

I'm waiting in the steaming, bubbling water when Heidi finally steps outside onto the deck. She sets two big, fluffy towels down. On top of the towels, she places the baby monitor, checking to make sure the volume's up. "Crap, it's cold."

"It's *invigorating.*"

"Invigorating my ass," she says, wrapping her robe tighter.

"Get in here and I'll warm you up."

She saunters closer and when she's almost within

grabbing distance, stops and whips her robe open. "What do you think?"

I think I should get her in the hot tub more often. "That's hot."

She turns and peeks at me over her shoulder. A sly smile curves her lips and she slowly lets the robe fall off her shoulders.

I guess technically it's a one-piece, but the red-hot suit's mostly backless except for a tie at the nape of her neck and strings that wrap around and tie in the middle of her back. The robe falls to the floor and she bends over, making sure to put extra wiggle in the move. The bottom of the suit is nothing more than a strip of material that barely contains her cute little ass.

"Turn around. Let me see the front again."

More thin strips of material connect the top and bottom.

"I can't see you well through all the steam. Come closer."

She narrows her eyes, as if she can sense my bullshit from two feet away. Finally, she steps up onto the platform and dips her toe in the water. "It's hot!"

"It's a *hot* tub."

"Ouch."

Instead of taking the plunge, she perches on the edge of the tub and slowly sticks her feet in. I glide over and kneel in front of her in the water, wrapping my arms around her legs. "Hey, pretty girl."

A soft smile lights up her face and she runs her fingers through my hair. "Hey."

"Aren't you cold?"

She peers down into the water. "You're not wearing a suit?"

"Come find out."

Her gaze darts around, as if she thinks we'll be caught at any minute.

"Rock and Hope aren't coming home tonight."

She slides into the water an inch at a time. "Ouch. Ouch. That's hot."

"It'll feel good in a minute."

"It better."

"Get over here." Under the water, I wrap my hand around her calf and drag her closer. Right into my lap.

She straddles me and loops her arms around my neck.

"For a girl who was worried about the forest creatures getting an eyeful a few minutes ago, you're feeling pretty bold." Under the water, my hands grip her thighs. My fingers stray to the edge of her suit, slipping under to stroke her skin.

"You like bold," she whispers.

"Yes, I do."

Cradling her head with one hand, I lean forward and brush my lips over hers. Her soft breath ghosts over my skin as I pull back. Her arms tighten around my neck and she dips down for another kiss.

I'm looking forward to a night of loud and lazy no-one's-home-to—overhear-us sex, so I take my time, slowly kissing her neck and shoulder. I drop my hand from the back of her head to the knot behind her neck and work it loose. The low-cut cups of her suit have been teasing the fuck out of me ever since she opened her robe. Beneath the water her hips rotate, pressing her pelvis into me until I groan.

I keep running my hands over the parts of her exposed to the night air, stopping to untie the other knot at the middle of her back. The suit falls forward and I stop to enjoy the sight. My hands cup her breasts and her head falls back. She gasps as I squeeze and caress. I rub my calloused fingers over her nipples and she grinds into my lap harder.

"Blake," she pants.

Under the water, I brush my knuckles against the fabric between her legs, stopping to press right over her clit several times.

"Blake," she whispers more urgently.

She's maybe five seconds from coming on my lap when the sound of voices infiltrates our steamy cocoon.

"Motherfucker," I grumble.

Heidi jumps back, moving to the other side of the hot tub.

For once, Wrath doesn't sneak up on me. His heavy boots thud over the deck loud enough to be heard over the bubbling water. I sit up right before he rounds the corner.

His mouth turns up in a smug, knowing smile. "Whatcha doin', kids?"

Heidi sinks lower into the water to retie the straps of her suit.

"What's it look like?" I growl.

"A lucky ginger who avoided a club party tonight," he says.

"How was it?"

Trinity taps his arm lightly and answers my question. "It was good."

"I didn't come over to talk about the party, though. I got a call earlier. We're back on track with the rebuild. Furious should be ready for a reopening this spring."

"No shit?"

"Keegan testified at the deposition. Insurance company musta figured it was stupid to keep fucking around."

"About fucking time."

"Amen, little brother."

"Talk to Whisper about it?"

"No, I wanted to tell you first."

I lift my chin at him. "Thanks."

Now that she's covered, Heidi floats over to me.

"We'll leave you guys alone," Trinity says, tugging on Wrath's arm. She mouths "sorry" to Heidi.

"I wasn't done," Wrath protests.

"Yes you are." In a lower voice, Trinity says something else that makes him follow her around the corner.

Rolling my eyes to the sky, I shake off the intrusion. "Where were we?" I ask, holding out my hand to Heidi.

She ducks her chin. "Can we go in the house?"

Inside, I'm groaning. Tomorrow, I'm punching Wrath as soon as I see him. "Sure."

My cock's hot and stone fucking hard, but the frigid night air takes care of that quick. Heidi throws a towel to me before wrapping one around herself.

"I'm going to take a shower," she says.

"Yeah, okay. I'll be there in a minute."

After closing the hot tub and shutting everything off, I

stop in our bedroom, not expecting Heidi to be in there getting dressed. "Thought you were taking a shower?"

"I rinsed off." She steps closer. "Why?"

"I wanted your wet, naked body in my hands."

She drops her gaze and reaches out to trace her fingers along the edge of the towel around my hips. "I'm still wet."

"Mind if I verify?"

She chuckles and hooks her finger in the towel, ripping it off. "Verify away."

With a loud growl, I pick her up and take the three steps to toss her on the bed. Laughing, she rolls over and sits up.

At the side of the bed, I drop to my knees and wrap my hand around one ankle, yanking her closer. "Put your pussy in my face."

She's not laughing any more. Holding my gaze, she hooks her thumbs into her flannel shorts and slowly drags them down before tossing them to the floor.

"Top too," I order.

That, she tosses at my face.

I catch it and throw it down. I kiss my way up the inside of her leg, stopping to lick behind her knees where I know it makes her flinch and laugh. Good and wedged between her wide-spread, toned legs, I kiss her hot pussy. And yes, she's still wet.

A happy noise rumbles out of me. She's sweet and tastes like heaven.

She tries to close her legs and jiggles with laughter. "Your beard tickles."

I flick my tongue over her clit with the soft feathery touch she needs at first.

"Oh," she moans. "That's so good."

"Still tickle?" I mumble.

"No."

I reach up, cupping her breasts, gently squeezing while I lick and suck until she's writhing on the bed.

"You couldn't do this outside," she whispers.

Answering requires taking my mouth off her and I don't want to do that, so I grunt in agreement.

"Blake," she whispers desperately. "I'm close."

I keep lapping and sucking. Her hands end up in my hair, grabbing and yanking. Her hips move in time with my kisses and I wrap my arms around her legs, pressing my hands against her belly.

I lick faster, harder, flick my tongue against her clit until her legs clamp around my damn head.

She screams a bunch of sounds. None of them are actual words. Love how I'm able to drive her mindless with pleasure.

She shudders and shakes as I ease back. I straighten up and swipe my hand over my mouth and chin. She's beautiful all spread out and flushed, a dreamy smile on her lips.

She raises her arms, reaching for me and I pull her up. She presses a quick kiss to my cheek. "Thank you."

I don't have a chance to answer because she crawls onto the bed, ass in the air. "I hope we're not finished," she says.

Don't need anymore encouragement than that. I rub the head of my cock against her slickness and she pushes back, gasping as I fill her to the hilt.

I grip her hips, angling her the way that works best for both of us.

Good. Fucking amazing, the way I fill her, hard and fast. Too fast. I want to take my time.

Slow Down. Enjoy.

Alexa's furious screams fill the air.

Stop.

Everything just *stops*.

"Shit." Heidi untangles herself from me. This isn't the first or even the tenth time something similar has happened. "I'll be right back. Stay there." She kisses my cheek. "I'm sorry."

Before she gets off the bed, I catch her hand. "Don't be sorry. I'll be here waiting."

She grabs my shirt and slips it over head, then races out the door.

"Fuck," I groan low enough she won't hear me. I don't want her to feel bad about something that's not even her fault.

Christ, my fucking balls hurt. I stand and stretch, then sit on the edge of the bed, stroking my cold, lonely, and confused cock.

What's probably only a few minutes later, but feels like an eternity, she returns, looking tired and definitely not in the mood to finish.

"Is she okay?"

"Everything's fine." She places her hands behind her back and leans against the door. "I just got a vivid reminder of what *this* leads to."

I snort. From now on I should be the one to go when this happens. There's not a damn thing that could dampen my desire for Heidi.

"All right." I stop stroking my cock so she sees I'm sincere. "I understand."

"Are you mad?"

"No." I'd been saving this for later, but now might work. "Hey, I got you something."

She quirks an eyebrow and drops her gaze to my dick.

"No, you already own that."

She chuckles. I hold out my hand and she takes it, sitting next to me on the bed. Without letting go, I reach over to the dresser drawer and slide it open, taking out a small rectangular box.

"What is it?" she asks.

It occurs to me that she probably won't know what it is, since I haven't found evidence that she already owns one. Figuring it's just easier to show her, I pluck it out of the protective foam and flick it on. The quiet whir fills the air between us as I lightly run it over her bare leg.

Her eyes widen with curiosity and maybe interest. "Is that a vibrator? What made you think I needed one?"

I will *not* tell her I walked in on Wrath when he was ordering Christmas presents at the clubhouse. He's already done enough to fuck up my night. "I thought it might be fun."

She cocks her head and stares at me for a minute. "You know you're enough for me, right?" Her eyes travel the length of me. "More than enough."

I give myself a few cocky strokes. "Trust me. I know."

She huffs out a short laugh. Her teeth sink into her bottom lip. "Maybe."

I brush her hair off her face and kiss her cheek. "You wanna just go to sleep?"

"I think so."

I stand and flip the light off, then gather her up and settle us under the covers. She curls up against me, resting her arm over my stomach. "Blake?"

"Yeah."

"Are you bored with me?"

"Fuck no."

She snuggles closer, her head on my chest, hand over my heart. One of my arms is curled around her, my hand absently stroking her hip. I'm too wound up to sleep any time soon.

My restless fingers keep moving and before I realize it, I'm stroking soft skin. She rolls closer, slinging her leg over mine and my hand drops lower cupping her butt.

"Blake?" she whispers.

"Hmm?"

"Will it hurt?"

"What?"

"The toy."

I turn, staring down at her. There's enough light to see her curious eyes blinking up at me. "Would I ever hurt you?"

"No."

I wait, eager but controlled, wanting her to make the decision.

"Let's try it."

It's hard—*ha!*—but somehow I manage not to jump out of bed and beat on my chest.

"I left it on the nightstand." Again, I want it to be her choice.

She twists her upper body, straining to reach the nightstand. We have a small light sitting on top of it that throws off a weak glow and she clicks that on before returning with the wand. A much more eager and interested expression brightens her face this time.

"It's so pretty and *cute*." She turns it over, checking it out.

Yeah, if it's her first one, I sure as shit wasn't going to buy some stainless steel eight-pronged monster vibrator to scare her with. This is pink and silver with little pink crystals studded along the handle. Almost innocent looking. *Almost.* Like Heidi.

"Show me," she says, handing it over.

I roll to my side, facing her. "Lie back."

She settles against the pillows. Even parting her legs, but I don't start there. I flick the switch and hold it in front of her face for a few seconds, then lower it to her breasts, still covered by my T-shirt. The second the little vibrating head makes contact she gasps.

"Oh!"

"Tickle?"

"Not exactly."

Her eyelids flutter shut and I take my time teasing both nipples to hard little points. I lean closer and take one between my teeth, using enough pressure to make her moan.

I glance up and find her watching me. "Take my shirt off?" she asks.

"Happy to."

She sits up, allowing me to drag the shirt up and over her head. Then my mouth's on hers. Slowly exploring and reconnecting.

"More," she whispers against my lips.

I pull back, staring down at her, admiring her flushed cheeks. Slowly, I drag the vibrator down her body. She laughs when it grazes her stomach. Gasps when I settle it right above her clit.

"Oh my God! Holy shit."

It's not manly to gloat, so I smother my smile and keep pleasing her. "How's that feel?"

"Good."

She grabs onto my arm, digging her nails in. "Blake. Oh. I." Her eyes close and her head falls back, her body jerking under me.

"That's it," I encourage in a low voice.

"I…" she gasps and her eyes pop open.

"What?"

"I need you. Inside me."

"Hold this," I say, placing her fingers around the wand. "Keep it right there."

"Fuck," she moans, arching her back as I push deep inside. I brace my arms by her shoulders, caging her in with my body. She lifts her hips, rocking her sexy fucking body against mine.

"How's that?"

She answers with a long moan that increases in volume with every thrust.

"Spread your legs. Let me see."

With a high-pitched moan she opens her thighs wider so

I can watch where our bodies meet. Stare at her hand rubbing the little wand over her clit.

"Good. So hot. So fucking good, Heidi."

"Uh. Yes."

I cover her with my body, grinding my hips against her, and fuck if the vibrations from that toy don't travel right down my dick.

She lifts her head to kiss me, moaning into my mouth. Endless cries and gasps. Her eyes roll back and she shudders hard. "Oh my God."

Tight. Fuck, I can feel every squeeze and flutter as she comes apart beneath me. I can't help following her and marveling at how good we are together.

Still breathing hard, she opens her eyes and stares up at me. The vibrations stop and she tosses the wand next to us. "You were right. That was fun."

Laughter bursts out of me and I kiss her forehead before pulling out. "Everything with you is fun."

The smile that lights up her face is my Christmas come early.

CHAPTER SEVENTEEN

Charlotte

"*Weeeee!*"

"Oh my God. What time is it?" I rasp without opening my eyes.

Marcel wraps one strong, warm arm around my waist, pulling me closer. "Merry Christmas," he murmurs, trailing kisses over my shoulder.

More baby giggles from across the hall make me smile. Marcel's laughter rumbles against my back. "I think Alexa's ready for Christmas."

"I can't believe she's awake so early when we were up until midnight making cookies for Santa," I whisper.

"She passed out and the grown-ups did all the work," Marcel reminds me.

The bed shifts and a few seconds later soft pink light pulls my eyelids open. Marcel swaggers over—bare torso on display and sexy boxer-briefs showcasing his impressive package—to the bed and wraps his hand around my ankle.

Slowly, he drags me to the edge of the bed. "Come on, to save time I'm going to give you your Christmas orgasm in the shower."

Outside our door, Alexa squeals again. Heidi shushes her which only makes Alexa yell louder.

Marcel doubles over, shaking with laughter. "She definitely takes after Heidi."

Scooting forward, I hook my finger in his waistband. "I believe you said something about a Christmas orgasm."

All teasing disappears and he focuses on me. "Yes, I did."

TELLER

AFTER CHARLOTTE and I exchange Christmas orgasms in the shower—*not* an easy feat when I'm pretty sure Blake was downstairs running all the hot water taps to hurry us along—we head downstairs.

"Morning!" Heidi shouts. She's blur of plaid flannel pajamas and wild hair as she barrels into me for a hug. "Sorry if we woke you up."

I squeeze her tight and muss her hair. “Sleep okay, bed head?”

She smacks my hand away with a smile. “You’ve got your own bed head going on, smart guy,” she says, jumping up to rub her hand over my head.

“Breakfast or presents?” Murphy yells from the kitchen.

“Better do breakfast first. Alexa won’t let you in another year or so,” Charlotte says.

“That’s what I thought too.” Heidi grabs Charlotte’s hand and then mine, dragging us into the kitchen. “That’s why I already started pre-heating the oven. I hope that’s okay?”

“That’s fine,” Charlotte says. “Thank you.”

Murphy has coffee poured for everyone, and after picking Alexa up and settling into one of the kitchen chairs, I heckle him for being so domesticated.

Charlotte narrows her eyes at me. “Are you trying to pretend you don’t have dinner ready almost every night when I get home from work?”

“Listen, ginger wonder-twins,” I say, pointing at the two of them. “No more of this conspiring nonsense.” I shift my gaze to Charlotte. “And *you*. What happens in our kitchen, *stays* in our kitchen.”

“Eee!” Alexa squeals.

“See, even Alexa agrees with me.”

Murphy grunt-laughs and slaps me on the back before setting a carton of creamer on the table.

Heidi hugs me from behind, wrapping her arms around my neck and practically choking me. “Aww, I knew my big brother would be good husband material for some lucky lady one day." She kisses my cheek before racing back to the stove.

"Lucky lady with the patience of a saint," Murphy adds.

"Da!" Alexa reaches for Murphy and he rubs a hand over her head. Then rubs his knuckles over *my* head.

"Knock it off," I mutter, slapping him away.

The loud chatter of my favorite girls and warm scents of Christmas breakfast fill the kitchen. Murphy takes the chair to my left and together we watch Charlotte and Heidi.

"Is Carter coming over?" he asks.

"I think so."

Charlotte turns around. "Bianca needed him to pick her up again last night." She rolls her eyes. "So she might be joining us too."

"You trust her?" Murphy asks me.

I shrug. I've only met the girl a couple times in passing. She seems nice enough.

"At our house, yes," Charlotte answers. "With my brother's heart, not so much."

Murphy snorts. "Is he interested in getting into her *heart* or her *pants*?"

"Ewww," Charlotte groans. "Both probably."

"Aww," Heidi sighs. "He's so sweet. I hope she's not using him."

Murphy shakes his head.

Breakfast is loud and delicious. Heidi makes this breakfast-bread-pudding thing that I'm sorry I teased her about last night when she prepped it.

"I can admit when I'm wrong, little sis. This was worth all the work you did last night."

"Thank you." She grins and pushes the glass dish my way again.

"Oh my God. You two need to stay over more often," Charlotte says. "I could get used to this."

Heidi laughs. "Then it wouldn't be as special."

After breakfast, Murphy and I clean up while Heidi takes care of Alexa and Charlotte brings presents downstairs. We meet up in the living room to exchange gifts.

"Marcel first," Heidi yells, dropping a sparkling green package in my lap. "Because you're the oldest."

"Actually, Charlotte is," I point out.

"That's okay." Charlotte waves her hand at me. "You go first."

"Careful," Heidi says, watching me intently.

Pushing layers of tissue paper aside, I uncover a heavy ten-inch blade. I grip it by the clearly custom-made blue and dark gray handle, turning it over. "Is it a Battle Mistress?"

"Yup."

Overwhelmed, I meet her eager eyes. "Heidi, it must have been really expensive."

Her cheeks flush. "I wanted to get you something nice. And I have a job now, you know."

Charlotte touches my side. "Holy shit, Heidi. I don't know if he can handle something so big."

Still a little choked up, I ignore Charlotte's teasing, even though I know it's her way of telling me to say *thank you* instead of questioning my sister.

"Blake said you lost your good hunting knife this year."

She gingerly takes it from me, testing its weight. "The guy I ordered it from said it's sturdy enough to behead a moose with."

I laugh and take it back from her. "We don't have moose around here."

She shrugs. "You never know."

I pull Heidi in and kiss her forehead. "Thank you. I really love it. I always wanted one. I didn't know they came in different colors."

Eyes sparkling and happy smile in place, she moves on to passing out other gifts.

Murphy and I don't usually exchange gifts. He and Heidi left their gifts for each other at Rock and Hope's, so soon we're on to spoiling the shit out of Alexa. Overwhelmed from the sheer number of toys and clothes we heap on her, she ends up passing out in a pile of wrapping paper. Heidi scoops her up, settling her daughter in her arms to watch her snooze.

This is the kind of Christmas I wanted Heidi to have when she was a kid. I always tried, but it never seemed good enough.

"You all right, bro?" Murphy says, sitting next to me.

"I'm glad you guys are here. Thanks."

"That's my gift to you," he jokes.

I tap the box with my knife in it. "You shouldn't have let her spend that much money."

"Shouldn't have *let* her? You've met your sister, right?" He takes the lid off the box. "I think Rock helped her order it. Did you notice the blade?"

I pull it out and examine it closer. Our club's skull and crown are engraved near the handle with my initials underneath.

"Wow."

"Yeah, so, you know, don't go gutting anyone with it."

I choke on a laugh and Heidi glances up. "What?"

"Nothing. Your boyfriend pointed out the engraving."

She rolls her eyes. "Fiancé. We're close to setting a date, you know."

"Your *old man* pointed out the engraving."

"*Wow*," Murphy says. "That might be the first time you've said it without turning green."

"Shut up." I shove him into the pile of pillows at the end of the couch and he jabs his foot into my leg. "Get your smelly feet off me."

He kicks me harder.

"Boys, please," Charlotte warns, breaking us up and sitting in between us.

Carter knocks on the side door and Charlotte gets up to let him in. I take the opportunity to tackle Murphy and wrestle him down to the floor.

We bump into Heidi, jostling Alexa awake and she lets out a scream, stopping both of us.

Heidi glares and holds out my niece. "You woke her, you can have her."

"Did I wake you, baby?" I ask in the mushy voice I only use with Alexa. She stops fussing and settles into my hold, reaching for one of her new toys.

Murphy pulls Heidi into his lap and she fusses over him like he just returned from battle.

"Whoa," Carter says, joining us. "Looks like Christmas exploded in here."

"Merry Christmas, Carter," Heidi says. Her gaze drops to Carter and Bianca's entwined hands and she grins. "You must be Bianca. Hi."

"Thanks for letting me join your family, Mr. Whelan," Bianca says. I can't tell if the breathy tone she uses is supposed to be sexy or the result of a hangover.

I'm not sure how I feel about being called *Mr. Whelan* or having this chick in my house, but it's Christmas, so I try not to be a grouch about it.

"Your sister's been waiting for you." I nod to a small stack of presents by the tree.

For a second it's awkward because I don't think anyone has anything for Bianca, but then Charlotte appears with a package. "I wasn't sure if I'd see you today or not," she says, handing it to Bianca.

"Thank you, Char."

A couple hours later, it's time to clean up and get moving. "I told Rock we'd be over by noon."

Heidi stands and wipes bits of paper off her legs. "I doubt they're up yet."

"I need to go to my parents'," Bianca says, turning to Carter. "You can join me."

"Uh," he glances at me. "I'm supposed to go—"

"You can show up whenever you want, Carter. No big deal."

I can't tell if he's relieved or he wanted me to give him an excuse for why he can't go.

Charlotte frets over it after they leave, until I pull her

aside. “He’s a big boy.”

“I know, I just don’t want him getting hurt.”

“He looked happy,” Murphy says.

“He looked *confused*,” Heidi corrects.

I nudge the girls toward the stairs. “Go start getting ready or we’re going to be late.”

Murphy shakes his head after they disappear. “Poor bastard. How’s he supposed to get laid with his sister right next door and in his business?”

“Maybe I should introduce him to some bunnies later.”

“No bunnies at the clubhouse tonight, bro.” He shakes his head. “No available ones anyway.”

“Come on. Let’s get ready. Rock’s gonna be annoyed if we’re late.”

ROCK

“Last present!” Hope calls out. She makes a big show of reading the tag, even though we wrapped it ourselves last night. “It’s for you, Heidi!”

“Me?” she asks, accepting the small box Hope hands her.

Teller glances at me and raises an eyebrow. I shrug as if I have no idea. While Heidi, Murphy, and Alexa spent the night at Teller and Charlotte's place, leaving Hope and I to a Christmas Eve alone—which we took full advantage of—they all showed up at the house before noon for Christmas brunch and gift unwrapping.

Intrigued by the box in Heidi's hands, Alexa crawls out of my lap and over to Heidi, plopping down in front her. "You want to help?" Heidi asks.

Alexa squees and rips at the paper, but Murphy scoops her up before she starts stuffing the bow in her mouth.

"Oh my God!" Heidi yelps. "Tickets to Country Fest?"

"Well, Murphy said you've never been to a concert," Hope says. "And I know you like Dawson Roads a lot."

"But these must have cost a fortune, Hope. They always sell out right away."

Hope just smiles. She'd gone to a lot of trouble and was pretty damn excited to score the tickets to the big country music festival that happens every year about an hour north of us.

"That's really cool. Thanks, Hope," Murphy says.

"Oh, wait." Heidi's eyes widen. "There're *four* tickets here."

Hope glances at Teller and Charlotte. "I figured you'd want to go with another couple or something."

"You don't want to come with us?" Heidi asks.

Well aware of my aversion to large, obnoxious crowds of drunk wanna-be cowboys, Hope waves the suggestion away. "You don't want the old couple tagging along."

"Hey." I poke her in the side.

Ignoring me, she continues, "Besides, we'll watch Alexa for you."

Heidi reaches over, hugging Hope. "Are you sure? You'll have enough of your own stuff going on this summer."

"I'm sure."

"If we can't, for some reason," I say, glancing at Hope. "You know Wrath and Trin will always watch her."

"I know. I just hate—"

Heidi's protest is cut off by the couple in question knocking, then coming in without waiting for an answer.

"Merry Christmas!" Trinity yells.

I stand and pull Hope up off the floor with me, so she can hug Trinity.

They have a bag of gifts for Alexa. She half-crawls, half-walks over to show off her bright red dress.

"Look at you in the fancy dress!" Trinity says, picking Alexa up and giving as many kisses as she receives. "Did Santa bring you lots of goodies?"

Alexa nods vigorously.

"Did you leave cookies out for Santa?" Wrath asks.

"Coo-coos!" Alexa giggles and points to our dining room table.

Trinity sets her down and Wrath hands over the bag. Alexa's thrilled to have more wrapping paper to shred and toss in the air.

"I think the *unwrapping* is her favorite part," Charlotte says.

Z's next to pop in and Alexa squeals in delight at the big red and white Santa cap he's wearing.

"That hat makes you look like a male stripper," Wrath says.

"Don't be jealous that I thought of it and you didn't," Z

quips, bending down to pick up Alexa and swing her around. "Are you having a good Christmas?"

"Yaya!"

"Oh my God," Heidi laughs. "I swore 'no' was going to be her answer to every question for the rest of her life. Thank you, Z."

Teller and Murphy help pick up the stray bits of paper and arrange all the opened presents under the tree.

"Clubhouse is packed," Z says. "Swan's got everything started in the kitchen, but I think she's waiting for you two." He nods to Trinity and Heidi.

"We were all about to head over," I say.

Charlotte groans. "I don't know if I can eat any more food today."

"Let me go put the tickets in my room," Heidi says. "So Alexa doesn't end up making confetti out of them."

"Good plan," Teller says.

Wrath, Trinity, and Z head over to the clubhouse first.

Hope runs upstairs to change and I follow.

"You're okay going over there for the afternoon, right?" I ask.

She stares at my reflection in the mirror while brushing her hair. "Of course I am. I've been looking forward to dinner with everyone."

I wrap my arms around her middle and pull her against me. "You look pretty, Mrs. North."

"Thank you."

Digging in my pocket, I take out one last present. "I have something else for you."

"I don't think we have time for you to show me your *pole* again, Mr. North."

Laughing so hard I almost drop the box, I shake my head. "No, you'll get my pole again later."

She opens the box and her eyes light up. "The North Star." She pulls out the heavy silver pendant with a solitary diamond in the middle. "Aww, it's beautiful."

"It matches your bracelet."

She lifts her arm to show me she's wearing the bracelet today. "I love it." She presses a kiss to my cheek. "It reminds me of *you,* lighting up our journey together."

"A constant reminder how much I love you," I add.

She turns and lifts her hair so I can slip the necklace around her neck and fix the clasp. "Thank you."

Downstairs, everyone's bundled up and ready to trudge through the snow to the clubhouse.

"Z cleared a trail earlier, but it's already getting covered over," Teller says.

"Well, we can always stay at the clubhouse if it keeps coming down this hard," Hope answers.

Murphy snorts at the look on my face. "I think Rock will shovel you a path home before he stays there."

"Amen to that," I mutter.

"Thnow! Tees!" Alexa yells twisting and turning in Murphy's arms. She yanks her hat off and tosses it at Teller. Her mittens go flying next and Heidi stops to pick them up.

"I don't know why I bother," she mutters.

"You did the same thing when you were her age," Teller says. "Karma never forgets."

"Shut up." A sneaky smile flashes across her face and she

stuffs Alexa's mittens in her pocket, then scoops up a handful of snow, balling it up and flinging it at Teller's back.

"Oh no you didn't, little sister!" he yells.

"Christ, keep walking, Charlotte, or you're going to end up covered in snow," Murphy advises, picking up his pace.

Keeping Hope out of snowball range isn't easy. "Knock it off, you two, before someone gets hurt," I growl as one goes flying past my face.

"Uh oh, who did Dad have to yell at now?" Wrath asks, popping up at the end of the trail.

"Shut up," Teller snaps, flinging the snowball he'd been preparing for Heidi at Wrath instead.

The ball of snow explodes against Wrath's chest and he calmly glances down and brushes the remnants off his coat. "Feeling suicidal today, little brother?" he asks in a grave tone.

Heidi runs ahead to catch up with Murphy. "Good luck with that, Marcel!" she shouts.

Charlotte rolls her eyes and stops to pat Wrath on the arm. "Do what you gotta do, big guy. I brought an extra change of clothes for him."

"What am I, five?" Tellers says.

"You *did* just lob a snowball at your big brother," Charlotte teases, sticking her tongue out at him.

"Do that again, woman. I have a better place for you to stick that tongue."

When we reach Wrath, Hope shakes her head. "Get him later when he least expects it."

An evil smile spreads across Wrath's face.

I groan and roll my eyes. "Why are you encouraging him, Baby Doll?"

Z's dogs are romping through the snow in front of the clubhouse. He throws a few snowballs and they race after them.

Inside the clubhouse isn't any less chaotic. The whole family's here. Even Charlotte's brother, Carter decided to join us.

Alexa's excited to see Bricks' and Winter's kids. Murphy sets her down to play but keeps a close eye on her.

Together, Hope and I work the living room. Making sure to check in with everyone. She even talks me into going downstairs for a tour of Sparky's latest crop—decked out in red Christmas balls. When the tour's over, Hope convinces Sparky and Stash to join us upstairs for dinner.

"Enjoy it now," I say before dinner. "We're going away for New Year's."

"Oh, really?"

"Yup. I'm thinking somewhere warm where you can prance around in bikinis for me all week."

"Mmm. I like the sound of that," she says, reaching up to kiss my cheek.

After dinner, I pull Hope's chair closer to me and curl my arm around her shoulders. "Did you have a good Christmas?"

She glances around the table at our extended Lost Kings family and smiles.

"The best one yet."

The End

AUTHOR NOTES

Thank you so much for purchasing and reading *One Empire Night!* I hope you enjoyed this peek at one night and one afternoon in the lives of the Lost Kings. I've wanted to write another collection of short holiday stories like *Three Kings, One Night* for a while.

It's an awkward time of year personally, as I know it is for a lot of people. While everyone else is busy putting up their trees and showing off their decorations, I'm usually cringing, waiting for the season to be over. I hate being one of those downer types who ruins the holiday for others, so I usually try to keep to myself.

The last two years, I've posted a Christmas card sign-up in my reader group. I wasn't sure I was going to do it again this year, because it ends up being a ton of work and way more expensive than I anticipate. I always say I'm going to cap it at a certain number, but I hate disappointing people and try to send out as many as I can, especially when I've come to recognize so many names on the sign-up list.

But then my readers started contacting *me* for my address. I went to my mailbox several times and found it so jammed with cards, I didn't think I'd get them out! It really helped me find my joy this year. My readers are the *best.* I receive some of the sweetest messages about how much you love my characters and how fast you've binge-read the series. Sometimes you share what *you're* going through and how my words have helped you through it and I really cherish those.

One Empire Night almost didn't happen. After the back to back releases of Teller's books, I was exhausted. I promised myself I'd take some time off, but then other things came up and although I wasn't getting my time off, I wasn't writing any new words either, which started to freak me out. But I couldn't resist the idea of Murphy, Heidi, Teller, and Charlotte taking Alexa to get her first Christmas tree. I loved Rock and Hope attending their very different parties together and being each others' support. Plus, I get asked about Mara and Damon a lot, so I wanted them to be there as well. Then, I posted a poll in my reader group about who they'd want to see a short story about. Rock was the winner by a *landslide.* Like, wow. That made me so happy. Then *someone* (Tanya, I know it was you!) added a "catch up with everyone" option to the poll, and that took the lead. Which was awesome, because that's sort of the turn the story was taking as Hope interacted with everyone at Crystal Ball.

I wrote *One Empire Night* for my core readers who really "get" me. And most of all, I wrote it for me. I loved catching up with everyone. I giggled every time I read the part where Murphy's waiting for Heidi to come back from changing Alexa, all the North Pole jokes, when Alexa makes a mess, Charlotte's lap dance, Wrath telling Trin he doesn't need porn, and most of all, the snow ball fight. When I first sent it to my crit partners, I said "it's really fucking sappy," but they loved it. My betas said it left them with the warm-fuzzies, and that was my goal.

My stories aren't conventional and I guess I write these notes to let you know, I'm aware of that. My deviation from what readers "expect" sometimes is intentional. I'm a firm believer in knowing the rules before you break them. So it's a conscious decision on my part. I talk about this endlessly with my crit partners and my writer friends. "I think I'm supposed to do *this* at this point in the story, but I don't *wanna* (yes, insert whiny writer voice there) and unless it's something major (like some of the loose threads I like to leave hanging) they usually tell me to go with my gut.

So, as I write this, it's a couple days before Christmas. I wanted to have *One Empire Night* on your e-readers *before* Christmas, but it needed more tweaks to get it right, so I hope you'll forgive me. While I'm typing these notes, Mr. Lake is sitting next to me stuffing envelopes with holiday cards to my readers. I'm looking forward to 2018 and what it will bring. I know what I *want* to write and publish. It will be interesting to see what actually ends up happening.

Thank you for supporting my work. Thank you for reading these notes.

I wish you the very best in the New Year.

xo

♡Autumn

ALSO BY AUTUMN JONES LAKE

Slow Burn (Lost Kings MC #1)
Corrupting Cinderella (Lost Kings MC #2)
Three Kings, One Night (Lost Kings MC #2.5)
Strength from Loyalty (Lost Kings MC #3)
Tattered on my Sleeve (Lost Kings MC #4)
White Heat (Lost Kings MC #5)
Between Embers (Lost Kings MC #5.5)
Bullets & Bonfires
Stand-Alone in the LOKI World
More Than Miles (Lost Kings MC #6)
White Knuckles (Lost Kings MC #7)
Beyond Reckless: Teller's Story, Part One (Lost Kings MC #8)
Beyond Reason: Teller's Story, Part Two (Lost Kings MC #9)
One Empire Night (Lost Kings MC #9.5)
Road to Royalty Boxed Set (Lost Kings #1-#3)*
Includes: Slow Burn, Corrupting Cinderella, Strength From Loyalty and a few bonus scenes not available in any of the other books.
*e-book only

Coming Soon:
After Burn (Lost Kings MC #10)
Zero Tolerance (Lost Kings MC #11)
White Lies (Lost Kings MC #12)

Catnip & Cauldrons Series*
Onyx Night
Onyx Shadows
Feral Escape
*ebooks only.

REQUEST FROM AUTUMN

Dear Reader,

If you loved *One Empire Night (Lost Kings MC #9.5)* (or any of my books,) please consider stopping by your favorite retailer, Book Bub, or Goodreads to leave a review. Reviews are so important for Indie Authors like myself. A few short lines is more than enough and greatly appreciated.

Thank you!

www.ingramcontent.com/pod-product-compliance
Lightning Source LLC
Chambersburg PA
CBHW061241170626
46809CB00007B/2767

* 9 7 8 1 9 4 3 9 5 0 2 7 0 *